SILLY SALAD

SILLY SALAD

A Collection of ice-breakers, games, and original skits

Amy K. Bond

iUniverse, Inc.
New York Lincoln Shanghai

Silly Salad
A Collection of ice-breakers, games, and original skits

iUniverse, Inc.

For information address:
iUniverse, Inc.
2021 Pine Lake Road, Suite 100
Lincoln, NE 68512
www.iuniverse.com

ISBN: 0-595-27857-4

Printed in the United States of America

To my brother Matt Lusk, and all the campers that he manages at Quaker Meadows Christian Camp in Springville, California.

My heartfelt thanks:
Once again to Becky Blair, without who's editing skills, I'd be looking very uneducated. Thank you Becky, I love you dearly!

To Linda Foersterling for all your diligent work on the word processor. I sincerely appreciate your help.

Shauna Gately and Jarri McClarin for the time they dedicated to proof-reading this book

To my dear friend Chris Lepley, for always letting me bounce even the craziest ideas off of her.

To my mom and dad for all of their input and ideas.

To my Grammie Carolyn for helping me to locate those hard to find bible verses.

To Pastor Lennie Spooner of the Baker City Nazarene Church for the use of all of your books, your encouragement, and your availability whenever I needed help on a scripture or interpretation of scripture.

To all my precious friends who put their reputations on the line to act out these skits and commercials in front of a live audience: Steve and Sharon Gibson, and their sons, Riley and Garret; Dean and Chris Barnes; Scott Ferguson; Lennie, Barry and Betty Spooner; David and Becky Blair; Vicki Williams; Anna Busch; Leah Michel; Erin Tucker; Alicia Fuzi; Carol Peterson; Erika Remple; Rick and Diny Michel (who ran sound and lights); Chris Zuercher and my husband, Clayton.

To the following friends who appear on the cover: Taryn and Brandon Suchy, Dean Barnes, Teresa Zuercher, Megan Berry, Becky Blair, Matt and Stacy Rex, and to my husband, Clayton, who shot the photo.

To my home church, Baker City First Church of the Nazarene, who encouraged me with their laughter and support.

To my precious family: Clayton, Reed and Reagan for their patience and support in allowing me to follow this dream.

Contents

Part III   COMMERCIALS, DISCUSSION STARTERS AND SKITS

PREFACE

Do you remember summer camp? I don't mean just church camp, but also cheerleading camp, leadership camp, music camp, tennis, baseball, basketball and volleyball camp? I do. Most of all, I remember that no matter what camp I was attending, there was always a moment of terror when my cabin or dorm was responsible for coming up with some kind of evening entertainment and it was always at the spur of the moment. Those were tough days. I never thought about it from the standpoint of the camp leader until I was asked by my church to come up with some variety show entertainment with virtuous messages for a Saturday night contemporary worship service.

Thanks to the willing participation of my good friends as actors, the material you will find in this book was tested before live audiences and chosen for its content and ability to inspire laughter. In addition, the response from the audience was very encouraging and got me to thinking about how these skits and commercials could be used by youth group leaders and youth camp counselors as a tool in teaching good living and God's word without sounding too preachy. Of course, I have my dear friends to thank for the success of this collection of diverse material. Without their help, I never would have believed how useful satire can be when presenting this kind of message. I hope you have as much fun acting it all out as we have.

INTRODUCTION

If you are a leader of teens or pre-teens, you know how difficult it can be to keep the atmosphere cool and happenin' while trying to slip in a message from God's word somewhere throughout the evening. It's tough! This collection of skits, games and ice-breakers are all original, although some inspiration was from old skits or games that I remember doing as a young camper. I hope I've brought them up to speed. What's better yet is that all these skits have been tested on a live audience and have produced laughter. The skits and commercials that you will find in this book, are followed by a scripture verse that explains what God's word really says as opposed to the skit and in essence, reveal its irony.

All but one of the skits and commercials combined are satirical, a "poking fun" at the wrong way to live or the misconstruing of God's word. The only serious skit I included is "Don't Know What You Got", which begins as comical but turns dark when the main character is not accepted into heaven due to his rejection of God while on Earth, therefore his name is not in the Book of Life. I feel this is the most important decision that a teenager can make. All the rest are forgivable, but where their Soul will spend eternity if they were to die today is very critical. At the very least, this skit will make them think about God as the Almighty giver of life and opportunity verses a disciplinarian who doesn't like anyone to have fun.

Before you get started on any of these skits I would like to suggest that you start collecting costume materials and props so that your materials will always be on hand when you need them. I found an ample supply of inexpensive wigs, hats, hideous glasses and fantastically outdated leisure suits at the local thrift store. Also, shopping through the costume isle the day after Halloween is always productive and inexpensive too. While you shop, think about how outrageous you can make the character "Dr. Meredith Stein", how absurd you can make the character "Samantha Super Christian", and how hilarious you can make "Bob and Bob". Sometimes it's costume alone that makes the act funny. I hope any youth group leader or camp counselor who uses this book will be pleased and that they will feel well equipped to teach and entertain with its contents.

PART I

ICE BREAKERS

ICE BREAKERS

Before any kind of interaction or discussion can take place between the members of your group, the ambiance of the meeting needs to be made casual and comfortable. Here are some suggestions of how to get the meeting off to a great start.

1. GROUP QUESTIONS

Ask any of these questions to the group; have them answer one at a time while going around in a circle.

A. Does your family include Santa Claus as part of Christmas? What will you do with your own family?

B. What song best describes you or your life? What is your theme song and why?

C. What historical figure do you most admire, and why?

D. If you saw someone being picked on by others and the scene was escalating, would you intervene? Why or why not?

E. Do you believe in guardian angels? Why or why not?

F. How do you think God speaks to people in modern times? Does He speak or inspire at all?

G. Do you believe that prayer can change another person's destiny? Can prayer touch God's heart enough to inspire Him to change His plans for someone?

H. Where do you think America is headed today in a spiritual sense? Are more people turning to Christ or to the World to answer tough questions?

I. What kind of parents do you think Han Solo had? (Other options: The Power Puff Girls, Shaggy from Scooby-Doo, Fred Flintstone)

J. Are you going to be more or less like your parents with your own children?

K. Where would be your ideal place to live, have a vacation home?

L. What would be your ideal career?

M. If you suddenly had 40 million dollars what would you do with the money?

N. Would you have liked to be born in another century? (The Dark Ages, the 1920's, 1950s, or have been a pioneer?) Why or why not?

O. Who is your favorite Sci-Fi character (Star Wars, Star Trek, Super Heroes) and why?

P. Which of the following would best describe your temperament? 1. Machine gun 2. A stick of dynamite with a short fuse. 3. A sparkler

2. MATCH-A-SONG

Everyone is given a small piece of paper with a common song on it (I.e. Mary Had a Little Lamb, Twinkle, Twinkle Little Star). When preparing for this icebreaker, write each song twice so there will be a match, a pair of people singing the same song. Then have participants find their partner by singing their songs all at once. This allows everyone to mingle with each other while searching for their partner. After everyone has found their partner, give them some time to get to know each other. At Christmas time, use common Christmas carols.

3. GETTING TO KNOW YOU WITH TOILET PAPER

A roll of toilet paper is passed around and everyone is to take as many squares as they like. When everyone has their squares tell them that they are to take their squares of toilet paper and approach someone else in the group that they know little about. Then they are to find out as many facts about that person as they have squares (if a person takes five squares-they have to find out five things about the person that they have paired with). Then, people are to report in front of the group what they discovered.

4. SPIDER WEB

Cut a long piece of string and tie the ends together so that it is a continual piece; judging the length of the string by the size of your group. Have all players hold the string around the outside of the circle of string. Then, one at a time, they are to cross the circle to someone on the other side. This won't work if the players go in order, so have players go in alphabetical order of their first names. Before too long you have a unique spider web made. Now try to untangle it by going backwards remembering who went in order, by name.

5. NAME GAME

Ask everyone to think of their favorite catch phrase, something they like to say, for example: "whatever!", "as if", "what's sup?", "Ooh la la", "yo baby", "bootie-licious") and have them write it on a name tag. Then they write their first name above it. Throughout the day or evening they are to be addressed by their name followed by the catch phrase (ie: Amy "yo mama").

6. FAMOUS QUOTES

Everyone is given a piece of paper with a famous quote on it. They are to find someone else who can identify who said the quote. Even if the person holding the quote knows who said it, they still have to find another person who can also identify it. Examples:

A. "May the Force be with you." (Luke Skywalker, Obi-wan, Yoda

B. "All we have to fear is fear itself." (Franklin D. Roosevelt)

C. "I have a dream." (Martin Luther King Jr.)

D. "Second star to the right and straight on till morning." (Peter Pan)

E. "Trust in me, just in me." (Kaa the snake—Jungle Book)

F. "Read my lips, no new taxes." (President George Bush Sr.)

G. "It's a good thing." (Martha Stewart)

H. "Let's roll." (President George Bush Jr.)

I. "I did not have sexual relations with that woman." (Bill Clinton)

J. "I cannot tell a lie." (George Washington)

K. "Let it be." (Paul McCartney)

L. "I can't get no satisfaction."(Mick Jagger)

M. "I am not a crook." (Richard Nixon)

N. "The Devil made me do it." (Flip Wilson)

O. "Bibbity, bobbity, boo." (Fairy Godmother from Cinderella)

P. "Toto, I don't think we're in Kansas anymore." (Dorothy—Wizard of Oz)

Q. "Only you can prevent forest fires." (Smokey Bear)

R. "Just say NO to drugs." (Nancy Reagan)

S. "Ask not what your country can do for you, but what you can do for your country." (JFK)

T. "We will bury you." (Khrushchev, president of Russia to USA)

U. "Pay me now or pay me later." (Pram oil filter)

V. "If I've told you once I've told you a thousand times." (Mom)

W. "Not by the hair on my chinny chin chin." (Three little pigs)

X. "What's up, Doc?" (Bugs Bunny)

Y. "Oh! A pic—a—nic basket." (Yogi Bear)

Z. "Heeeeerrrres, Johnny." (Ed McMahan)

AA. "You deserve a break today." (McDonalds)

BB. "Come on down, you are the next contestant on the Price is Right." (Rod Roddy)

CC. "D d d da that's all folks!" (Porky Pig)

DD. "Kids! I am going to count to three!" (Mom)

EE. "Fly the friendly skies." (United Air Lines)

FF. "The sky is falling, the sky is falling!" (Chicken Little)

GG. "Get a piece of the rock." (Prudential Insurance)

HH. "Like a rock." (Chevrolet)

II. "Because so much is riding on your tires." (Michelin)

JJ. "Eating good in the neighborhood." (Applebee's)

KK. "My, what big teeth you have!" (Little Red Riding Hood)

LL. "I got no strings." (Pinocchio)

MM. "Hi ho, hi ho, it's off to work we go." (Seven Dwarfs)

NN. "A mind is a terrible thing to waste." (United Negro College Fund)

OO. "Doesn't it feel good to pay less?" (PayLess Drug Store)

PP. "Who you gonna call?" (Ghost Busters)

QQ. "Don't leave home without it." (American Express)

RR. "Diamonds are a girl's best friend." (Carol Channing or Marilyn Monroe)

SS. "Master the possibilities." (MasterCard)

7. MATCH THAT QUOTE

A variation on Name That Quote would be to Match That Quote. Instead of finding someone who can name the owner of the quote, give half of the group a piece of paper with the quote on it and the other half a piece of paper with the owner of the quote on it and have them mingle and match up that way.

8. WHO'S THE MOST LIKELY TO…

After your group has had some time to get to know each other, this ice-breaker is a fun way to loosen everyone up. Split the group into smaller groups of six or seven and have them discuss and decide what each one of them would most likely be doing with their lives if they were all to reunite twenty years from now. Here are some choices:

A. Have written a best-selling romance novel based on their own love life.

B. Have fifteen children and live in a giant shoe.

C. Be a body builder with their own line of muscle-building powdered drinks and portable exercise accessories for toning "abs" and "glutes".

D. Be a dance instructor on a cruise ship.

E. Have retreated in to the backwoods of northern Idaho and live in a self-constructed log home, entering town for supplies only once per month and never installing a telephone.

F. Be a professional bowler with their own line of bowling shoes, each inscribed with their name on the sole.

G. Have their own radio talk show where they discuss conspiracy theories with callers who say they have the "inside track" concerning the goings on of the world.

H. Be a food scientist who actually develops a non-nutritive food additive that actually keeps cereal crunchy in milk.

I. Be a politician who is an outspoken follower of Christ.

J. Win the ten million dollar prize on "America's Funniest Home Video's" for being caught on tape falling out of a boat.

K. Have a front tooth capped in gold.

L. Missing one or more front teeth…for whatever reason.

M. Be a wild animal trainer for a Hollywood producer.

N. Own and produce an adventure series on cable called "Freaky Planet".

O. Be a "before and after" model for a hair club hair re-growth commercial, and not to mention, the president of the club.

P. Organize animal rights protest marches and suspect in several investigations concerning the mysterious releasing of hundreds of lab mice across the U.S. from testing laboratories.

Q. Discover multiple uses for "Preparation H".

R. Lose a finger while inventing "The Perfect Mousetrap".

S. Get a tattoo at a biker rally.

T. Be a parachuting Elvis impersonator in Vegas.

9. WHICH CELEBRITY ARE YOU?

Place a piece of paper on every player's back that has the name of a celebrity on it. Players are then to mingle and ask questions of each other that can only be answered with a "yes" or a "no" about who they are. For example; "Am I male?" "Am I female?" "Do I have blond hair?" "Do I have hair?" After asking three questions, the person is to move on to someone else until they determine which celebrity they are.

If you would rather, use Bible characters rather than celebrities, and as an additional spin, once the players determine who they are, have the Bible characters pair up as they do in the Bible. For example: Samson and Delilah, Mary and Joseph, David and Goliath, and so on.

10. GOOD DEED BINGO

All players are given a pencil and the grid as seen below.

Have the participants mingle about, asking others if they have carried out any of the good deeds that are listed in the boxes within the past month. When a player finds someone that fits the criteria in one of the boxes, the player can fill in the box. A bingo can be achieved either horizontally, vertically or diagonally.

When a player has filled seven consecutive boxes and yells out "Bingo!" the game is over.

Wiped A Nose	Said Hello to A Stranger	Shook Someone's Hand	Visited someone Who is Sick	Chopped Someone's Firewood	Prayed for Someone	Bought A Gift
Mowed Someone's Lawn	Folded Laundry	Changed A Diaper	Walked A Dog	Cooked A Meal	Read A Book To A Child	Threw A Party
Went To Church	Drove Someone To Church	Visited A Grade-School	Visited A Hospital	Volunteered In Sunday-School	Gave A Baby A Bottle	Played With A Toddler
Raked Leaves	Told Someone You Love Them	Placed A Band-Aid On Someone	Shoveled Snow	Sang In Church	Played An Instrument In Church	Gave A Beggar Your Change
Tithed At Church	Gave To A Charity	Volunteered At A Shelter	Volunteered At A Soup Kitchen	Bought Someone's Lunch	Fed A Stray Animal	Picked Up Litter
Wrote A Note To Encourage Someone	Verbally Encouraged A Friend	Gave Someone A Hug	Coached A Sport Team	Cheered For The Underdog	Shared Your Lunch	Gave Your Testimony
Shared Your Faith With Someone	Changed A Tire For Someone	Stopped To Help Someone In Trouble	Babysat For Free	Worked In Church Nursery	Kept A Secret	Held A Baby

PART II

GAMES

GAMES

1. WINK'UM

An odd number of players is best. Arrange chairs in a circle facing inward. For as many players that you have, divide them in half and add one, which will give you your desired number of chairs needed. While leaving one chair empty, have half of your players sit in the remaining chairs. The rest of your players are to stand behind your seated players with their hands behind their backs (note: one chair will be empty, with a standing player behind it). To begin the game, the standing player who is without a seated partner, is to wink at someone who is seated. The person who was signaled by the wink is to immediately leave their chair and come to sit in the empty chair. The trick is for that person to leap from their chair before the standing player behind them reaches out to tap them on the shoulder. What makes this game so fun is that it needs to be done without speaking, only winking.

2. "IMPROV" AT A PARTY

Four players from the group are selected to begin.

Each player is given an unusual personality to act out in a party setting. The first player is the host of the party. The audience is to guess what/who the players are pretending to be. When the unusual personalities are all guessed, a new group of four players is selected with new personalities to act out.

UNUSUAL PERSONALITY SUGGESTIONS:

*Slug whose been doused in salt

*Paranoid Pirate

*Invisible man/woman

*Mad scientist

*Talk show host

*Used car salesman

*A destructive 3-year-old

*Butterfly coming out of its cocoon

*"Ginger" from Gilligan's Island

*Angry badger

*Piece of bacon in a fry pan

*Stray dog

*Over-zealous policeman

*A person with several personalities

*A super hero

*A lion tamer

*A gymnast

*Fred Flintstone

*Dracula

*A newborn baby

*Fish on a hook

*Pyromaniac

*A Jedi

*A "clean" freak

3. FILL IN THE BLANK

Two teams of players are established. One player from each team comes to the front to sit in the hot seat. Everyone is given paper and pencils. The entire group must privately answer a fill-in-the-blank question by writing it on their paper.

Then, the two in the hot seat are asked to reveal their answers and the team that has the most matches with the one player in the hot seat gains a point. The players in the hot seat can be rotated around with the rest of the players.

SUGGESTIONS OF "FILL-IN-THE-BLANK" QUESTIONS

A. Liz fell asleep with chewing gum in her mouth. When she awoke, she found her gum in her_____.

B. _____ is the term I use to describe newlyweds on their honeymoon.

C. The last time I saw Cliff, he had a _____ on his face.

D. After I had entered my school, I was surprised to find that I had stepped in _____.

E. Never before had Carol seen such a _____ at the ballet.

f. Opera wasn't Hank's bag. He would rather have been _____.

G. Waiter! There's a _____ in my soup!

H. Mary had never been good at multi-tasking, so her _____ lessons were very difficult.

I. Playgrounds are so dirty that every time my children play at one they catch a _____.

J. When we got home, we were horrified to see that our _____ got loose.

K. After dark Jim's favorite pastime is to _____.

L. Never underestimate the power of the _____.

M. A _____ can be talked into anything.

N. Earl emerged from the restroom, embarrassed, when his _____ had gotten stuck in his zipper.

O. Never before had Fred seen such _____ on another person.

P. Mark's mouth hung agape, when out of the sky emerged _____.

Q. Jim-Bob rode his _____ all around the barnyard.

R. Housework and _____ don't mix.

S. The last time I went camping I saw a _____ catch a rodent.

T. She thought she might _____ when she discovered she had swallowed a fly.

4. NAME THAT BIBLE PERSONALITY

Two teams of players are established with a spokesperson for each team. Clues which outline a person from the Bible, are given to both teams. Only one team at a time is allowed to answer. If the first team can't answer the question, the second team can try to answer. With each correct answer, that team earns their points with no more than five clues given. If a team can identify the Bible personality from one clue, they will earn five points. If they can identify the Bible character in two clues, they earn four points, in three clues—three points. In four clues—two points and in five clues—one point. Fifteen seconds for discussion is allowed after each clue is given.

SUGGESTIONS FOR CLUES

1. NOAH

    a.   Was thought to be a mad man by his peers

    b.   He was blameless among the people of his time

    c.   Had three sons, Shem, Ham, and Japheth

    d.   Collected two of every animal to go on the ark

    e.   Built a big boat

2. JONAH

    a.   Never really understood what God was trying to teach him

    b.   Was a prophet in the Old Testament

    c.   Hated the people of Nineveh

    d.   Set sail off the Joppa coast

    e.   Was swallowed by a giant fish

3. GOLIATH

    a.   Was mean by nature

    b.   Had five brothers

    c.   Was a Philistine

    d.   Was approximately eight feet tall

   e.   Was defeated by David

4. JOHN THE BAPTIST

   a.   Visited the temple with Jesus

   b.   Son of Elizabeth & Zacharias

   c.   Was Jesus' cousin

   d.   Baptized Jesus

   e.   Ate locust and wild honey

5. DAVID

   a.   Was a young shepherd

   b.   Had great faith in God

   c.   Had seven brothers

   d.   Tried to wear King Saul's armor

   e.   Was deadly with a sling shot

6. RUTH

   a.   Widowed when she was still young

   b.   Came from Moab, a people who were idolaters.

   c.   First husband's name was Mahlon, meaning "invalid or the sickly one"

   d.   Second marriage was to Boaz

   e.   Vowed to always care for her Mother-in-law, Naomi

7. JACOB

   a.   Tricked his ailing father into giving him his brother's blessing

   b.   Had two wives, Rachel & Leah

   c.   Had a twin brother named Esau

   d.   Original name means "deceiver", new name means "wrestled with God"

e.   God changed his name to Israel. He walked with a limp

8. MOSES

a.   Talked with an embarrassing stutter.

b.   Was a shepherd in Midian.

c.   Prayed fervently for God's mercy—not to destroy the Israelites.

d.   Wrote the Ten Commandments.

e.   Parted the Red Sea.

9. SAMUEL

a.   God spoke to him as a boy, through visions, voices

b.   Was raised by Eli, his foster father

c.   Mother was Hannah

d.   Became a judge of Israel

e.   Led Israel to victory over the Philistines

10. JOSHUA

a.   Born a slave in Egypt

b.   Conquered Canaan

c.   Was a spy

d.   Took over leadership of the Israelites after Moses died

e.   Fought the battle of Jericho

11. SAUL

a.   Was made King by Samuel

b.   Jealous of David, tried to kill him

c.   Turned away from God—consulted a witch for guidance

d.   Leadership and life became failures, defeated in battle

e.   Committed suicide

12. SOLOMON

    a.   Had 700 wives and 300 concubines

    b.   Built God's temple

    c.   Raised in the palace amid great family turmoil

    d.   Son of David and Bathsheba

    e.   Chose wisdom over power

13. MARY MAGDALENE

    a.   Her name identified her place of birth

    b.   She had no family, husband or obligations

    c.   Was tormented by seven demons

    d.   Was a prostitute

    e.   Was present at the crucifixion of Jesus

14. JAMES

    a.   Was one of the twelve disciples

    b.   His grave, which was uncovered in 2002, had Jesus' name written in stone on it—marked an enormous archeological discovery

    c.   Was stoned to death as a Jewish Heretic in A.D. 62

    d.   Head of the Jerusalem Church in his time

    e.   Was Jesus' half-brother

15. ELISHA

    a.   Selected by God as a prophet

    b.   Grew up on a farm.

    c.   Served ten years in ministry

    d.   Continually confronted Ahab & Jezebel of their wrong doing

    e.   Succeeded Elijah as God's special prophet

16. DANIEL

a.   Grew up in Judah in a noble and godly home.

b.   Served under Nebuchadnezzar in the Babylonian court.

c.   Interpreted Nebuchadnezzar's dreams.

d.   Promoted to high priest of Babylon.

e.   Stayed loyal to God even under Persian rule, which landed him in the lion's den.

17. JESUS

a.   Was never married or settled down

b.   Learned the trade of a carpenter from his stepfather

c.   Performed miracles, healed the sick, raised the dead

d.   Died at the age of 33

e.   Crucified on a cross at Calvary

18. TIMOTHY

a.   Became a Christian under St. Paul's ministry

b.   An apprentice of St. Paul

c.   His health was poor, described as "sickly by nature"

d.   Co-authored the Book of Philippians, Colossians & Philemon

e.   Was commanded by Paul to remain in the disorderly & crumbling church in Ephesus, but he didn't want to, this person struggled with being content

19. VIRGIN MARY

a.   Her name is so revered that it is the only feminine name with pronounced masculine forms

b.   Her name occurs 51 times in the New Testament

c.   She was from tribe of Judah, line of David, but was a Nazarene

d.   Her baby was not of her husband

    e.   Mother of Jesus

20. BATHSHEBA

    a.   Name means the seventh daughter.

    b.   Her first husband was Uriah, who was murdered.

    c.   Her father was one of King David's gallant officers.

    d.   Mother of five sons with her second husband.

    e.   Famous for her adultery with King David.

21. JOSEPH

    a.   Had six brothers

    b.   Sold into slavery

    c.   Imprisoned after being falsely accused of rape

    d.   Could interpret dreams

    e.   Became high priest of Egypt

22. DELILAH

    a.   Name means delicate, or dainty one, coveted name among women of her time

    b.   Through her evil deeds, her name became shameful and associated with guilt. No other woman bears her name in the Bible. It is rare to find a woman with this name

    c.   Used her charm and beauty for only one purpose—to get money

    d.   Betrayed her lover for silver

    e.   Husband was Samson

23. ELIZABETH

    a.   Name means worshiper of God

    b.   Came from a prestigious family of priests, daughter of Aaron

    c.   Laughed when God's messengers said she would have a baby

    d.   Wife of Zacharias the priest

   e.   Had a baby "John" in her old age

24. ESTER

   a.   Name means star of hope

   b.   The last woman of the Old Testament

   c.   Concealed her nationality from the king

   d.   Her marriage to the king was against the law

   e.   Became queen at a young age, but just in time to save the Jews from destruction

25. EVE

   a.   The first woman to be called "a wife"

   b.   The first mother to have a son who was a murderer

   c.   The first woman to be assailed by Satan

   d.   Mother of Cain and Abel

   e.   Wife of Adam

26. MICHAL

   a.   Is known for deceiving her father and forsaking her husband

   b.   The younger daughter of King Saul

   c.   Never conceived children but cared for her sister's five children, all of whom were beheaded

   d.   Was disgusted with her husband's display of praise to God

   e.   Despised her husband, King David

27. NAOMI

   a.   Name means pleasant, changed her name to Mara which means bitter

   b.   Widow of Elimelech

   c.   Her two sons were Mahlon and Chilion

   d.   Begins life in comfort and luxury, plummets to poverty

    e.   Mother-in-law of Ruth and Orpah

28. SAPPHIRA

    a.   Name means Sapphire

    b.   She and her husband agreed to lie against God.

    c.   Theirs was the first act of deceit in the newly formed church.

    d.   With her husband, they schemed to look like they gave the whole price of the piece of land that they sold to the church so they would be held in high esteem.

    e.   Dropped dead about three hours after her husband when she was confronted by Peter with their sin.

29. SARAH

    a.   Known as the woman who became the "Mother of Nations".

    b.   She and her husband were children of the same father but different mothers

    c.   Abraham's wife.

    d.   Was part of Pharaoh's harem as part of a deceptive plot to save Abraham's life.

    e.   Was 90 years old when she bore Isaac.

30. ZIPPORAH

    a.   One of the seven daughters of Jethro

    b.   Moab name meaning "little bird"

    c.   Father was high priest of Midian

    d.   Did not share the spiritual values of her husband

    e.   Wife of Moses

5. BODY SURFING

Everyone can participate. All players lay face down, side by side and in a line, on the floor or grass if played outdoors. The first player on the far left of the line lays on top of the other player at the left end. Simultaneously, all of the players who are laying down, roll to *their* left continually moving the player on the top across the rest in a wave like movement. When the first body surfer is about halfway across, another surfer can begin from the far left, as each surfer reaches the end of the wave of rolling players, they lay on down next to the player on the far right and roll right along also, then leaving the role of the surfer and becoming part of the wave.

6. WHERE IS HERKAMER?

Herkamer is a character that can be of your own creation, but must consist of a small drawing on a circular piece of paper that has been laminated so that it can be easily slipped into someone's pocket unnoticed.

A counselor or group leader can begin with Herkamer and at some time throughout the time period in which you're meeting, the counselor must slip Herkamer into someone's pocket unnoticed. At dinner time (if at camp) or at the finale of a youth group meeting, a special little song can be sung to set up the revealing of Herkamer. The lyrics are as follows and is sung to the tune of Michael Finnegan:

"Where, oh where is our little Herkamer,
Where, oh where is our little Herkamer,
Where, oh where is our little Herkamer,
Way down yonder in somebody's pocket."

While the song was sung all members check their pockets. When someone discovers Herkamer in their pocket, they must come to the front of the group and do something embarrassing. I suggest the "Chicken Dance". *Note*: If a player discovers Herkamer in their pocket before the evening get together, they can avoid the embarrassment of the "Chicken Dance" by placing Herkamer into someone else's pocket.

7. TAKERS AND RETURNERS

For a camp setting—each bunk-house has a designated flag or mascot which represents their group. If any other bunk-house can take that mascot or flag without being caught, they are to keep their thievery a secret until dinner where their deed will be revealed.

The mascot or flag will then be presented to a neighboring bunk house who will have to return the object within the next twelve hours, again without being caught doing so.

For a youth group—not all youth groups have a flag or mascot. If yours does, play the game in much the same way as explained before, requiring the object to be returned within a week's time (since these groups often meet weekly).

Or

Designate an object from your youth group room (hot cocoa can), eraser, etc, and challenge anyone to take it and keep it in a safe hiding place. In turn, anyone else can look for the object and take it away from the first taker only to hide it themselves. The challenge can go on and on for a designated period of time. The last person to have the object wins.

8. SEEK AND GO HIDE

A large group can play. One person goes and hides somewhere in a designated area and everyone else goes to look for that person. Each time a person finds the one hiding, they hide with them until all the seekers are hiding and can begin again.

9. KICK THE CAN

A large group can play. You need an empty coffee can. All but one player goes out into darkness to hide. One person stays with the can, guarding it from being kicked. Any of the players who are out creeping around can sneak up on the guard of the can and kick it. If the guard sees them in time to call out "over the can on Sam!" (or whoever the person is by name) while the guard steps over the can, the person who was spotted is put in "jail" or has to sit down by the can. If a player is able to kick the can while others are in jail, all the jailed players are free and can run off into the darkness. The guard-of-the-can is relieved when all the players are in jail or when the guard is frustrated and quits.

10. QUESTION, QUESTION

This game was inspired by Shakespeare's jolly but dim-witted characters, Rosencrantz and Guildenstern from the tragedy "Mac Beth". My best friend in High School and I used to play this game as we went up the ski lift, laughing all the way.

Two teams of players, one player from each team competes at a time. The two players face each other and ask each other questions, responding only with other questions. If a player responds to the other with a statement then they are out and the next player from their team will take their place. If a player responds with a question that is rhetorical or a copy of what the first player has already said, they are not out, but the other team will receive two points. One point will also be given to the other team when a player responds with a word or phrase that doesn't exist, for example:

Player 1: "Do you want to play a game of questions?"
Player 2: "Are you talking to me?"
Player 1: "Are you hard of hearing?"
Player 2: "Huh?"

"Huh?" although an appropriate response in this situation, is not a real word. Player 2 would not be out but Player 1's team would receive one point. The game is over when all players have been rotated through and the points are tallied. The team with the most points wins.

11. MOOSE, MOOSE

Six to eight players are required. Each player is given an animal to imitate with sound and gestures. Six, seven or eight players stand side by side with person #1 beginning with their designated sound and gesture, followed by the sound and gesture of someone else in the line. That person in turn does his or her designated sound and gesture, followed by someone else's and so on. When someone messes up the order, he/she is out; the group shifts one spot to the right, and takes on a new animal sound and gesture. The game is over when everyone has rotated into the line and the person remaining at position one is the winner.

Animal sounds and gestures are as follows:

Sound	Gesture
Position #1 "Moose, moose"	Hands out at ears like Bullwinkle.
Position # 2 "Quack, quack"	Two hands together to make a bill.
Position #3 "Cluck, cluck"	Fists under arms like chicken wings.
Position #4 "Boing, boing"	Jump with hands in front like kangaroo.
Position #5 "Eek, eek"	Scratch under armpits like a monkey
Position #6 "Hee haw, hee haw"	Kick one leg backward like a donkey.
Position #7 "Squeak, squeak"	Wiggle nose and ears like a mouse.
Position #8 "SSSS, SSSSS"	Wiggle hands together like a snake.

PART III

COMMERCIALS, DISCUSSION STARTERS AND SKITS

COMMERCIALS

Commercials are nothing more than very short and easy skits. Fewer people are needed and so is very little practicing. If you need a quick intro to a topic, these commercials will serve you well.

1. FENCE-SITTER'S FANNY PAD (a commercial on indecision)

Players:	Two; the Fence Sitter and the Announcer
Props:	Pillow
	Makeshift fence (two chairs with a board across them to mimic a fence)

Opening scene: One player is behind the scenes acting as the announcer. The other is in front acting out the commercial. They begin by sitting on the makeshift fence, just passing the time away.

THE FENCE SITTER'S FANNY PAD

Announcer: Has this ever happened to you? You just get settled in and...

Fence Sitter: Ouch! I've got a sliver in my bottom!

Announcer: And that's not all, the bruising, the chafing, the all-around discomfort involved when you live your life sitting on the fence. Don't go to extremes; don't jump with both feet into a life for Christ. You can stay on that fence with the help of *THE FENCE SITTER'S FANNY PAD*.

(The Fence Sitter reaches down and retrieves a pillow. He then puts the pillow under his bottom, and sits back down on the fence.)

Announcer: Can you imagine sitting-the-fence for the rest of your life, only in comfort? It can be yours with only three small payments of $9.95 plus shipping and handling. Because life is full of indecisions and you can make the *Fence-sitter's Fanny Pad* work for you by decreasing the life-long wear and tear on your bottom that those indecisions can cause.

Fence Sitter: *(giving a "thumbs up sign" with right hand)* Thanks *Fence-sitter's Fanny Pad.*

Announcer: Brought to you by King of Lies Industries and DEVIL Products, Inc.

Scripture reference: Revelation 3: 15-16 "I know your deeds, that you are neither cold nor hot. I wish you were either one or the other! So because you are luke-warm—neither hot nor cold—I spit you out of my mouth."

2. GOOD DEED ORGANIZER (a commercial on good works)

Players:	Two; the Actor and the Announcer
Props:	A large accordion file or three-ring binder
	A small folder

Opening scene: One player acts as the announcer while the other acts out the commercial. As the announcer begins his monologue, one actor is sitting thought-fully, in front of the audience.

GOOD DEED ORGANIZER

Announcer: Do you want to get to Heaven? Do you want to get there faster than anyone else? Do you want to be held in the highest esteem when you get there? What you need is the *Good Deed Organizer.*

(Actor displays the organizer)

The *Good Deed Organizer* will help you keep track of all your good deeds, so when you arrive at the pearly gates of heaven you can prove your worthiness! Order now, and as a bonus gift, we'll also include the *Thank You Note Tote* (*actor displays the tote*) so you can keep track of those who have acknowledged your kindness and those who didn't. Because, the ticket on the train to heaven isn't free, it's paid for in works.

Actor: (*giving a "thumbs up sign" with right hand*) Thank you *Good Deed Organizer*!

Announcer: Brought to you by King of Lies Industries and DEVIL Products, Inc.

Scripture reference: Ephesians 2: 8 *"For it is by grace you have been saved, through faith—and this not from yourselves, it is the gift of God—not by works, so that no one can boast."*

3. THE BURDEN MASTER (a commercial on carrying the weight of the world on your shoulders).

Players:	Five; Mom, Daughter, Son, Father and Announcer
Props:	Broom or mop
	Backpack with two large sheets or duvet cover pinned to it to appear like a layer backpack. As the commercial progresses and each player comes out to say their piece, they enter the burden master by hopping inside the two sheets.

Opening scene: As the announcer begins his monologue, the mother is seen fervently mopping the floor, holding her aching back.

THE BURDEN MASTER

Announcer: Vacuuming, dishes, laundry and mopping. It's hard enough to keep up your home but when you have worries and troubles dragging you down, it can be almost impossible! Struggle no more! Introducing *The Burden Master*! A revolutionary mixture of American design and European engineering that allows you to actually carry your burdens and still accomplish household chores. Just watch what the *Burden Master* can do for you:

Daughter: Mom, I don't care that he's 38 years old, we love each other.

Mom: It's okay hon., hop in the back.

(*Daughter enters into the extended backpack. Father enters into scene*)

Father: Honey, if we don't find some money by Monday, we'll have to declare bankruptcy.

Mom: Don't worry about it babe, just hop in the backpack.

(*Father enters into the extended backpack, son enters into scene*)

Son: Mommy! Spot is foaming at the mouth and chewing the bark off our tree!

Mom: I can handle it, son, come on in.

(*Son enters into the extended backpack*)

Announcer: Because when you have the weight of the whole world to carry on your very own shoulders, you need the *Burden Master.*

Mom: (*giving a "thumbs up sign" with right hand*) Thank you *Burden Master.*

Announcer: Brought to you by King of Lies Industries and DEVIL Products, Inc.

Scripture reference: Matthew 11: 28-30 "Come to me, all you who are weary and burdened, and I will give you rest. Take my yoke upon you and learn from me, for I am gentle and humble in heart, and you will find rest for your souls. For my yoke is easy and my burden is light."

4. SIN-NO-MORE SPECTACLES (a commercial on adultery)

Players:	Four; Announcer, Husband, Wife, and a Hot Babe
Props:	Ugly glasses
	A ladies purse
	A hideous mask used to quickly transform the "Hot Babe" from lovely to ugly.

Opening scene: As the Announcer begins to speak, the husband and wife are walking arm in arm across center stage.

SIN-NO-MORE SPECTACLES

Announcer: Are you tired of your wife catching you lusting over other women? Are you exhausted from the amount of self-control you have to practice from day to day at work, the gym or even in the hardware store?

The Sin-No-More Spectacles can help! Just place the *Sin-No-More Spectacles* over your eyes like regular glasses and watch your life change. Finally, you'll be living the life you're pretending to live every Sunday at church. Not only that, we guarantee your wife will thank us! Just watch how the *Sin-No-More Spectacles* can work for you…

(Hot Babe enters, catches the husband's attention, wife notices and whacks him with her purse. After a few whacks, the husband gets smart and places the glasses on his face. Meanwhile, the Hot Babe exits and changes quickly into the ugly costume.)

Announcer: When you are presented with visually stimulating temptation, put on the *Sin-No-More Spectacles.* Not only will the member of the opposite sex look unattractive, but they'll look down right hideous!

(Hot Babe returns as a monster, husband responds accordingly.)

Announcer: Because every married man knows that the key to a successful marriage is a happy wife, and self-control can sometimes be too much to ask.

Husband: (giving a "thumbs up sign" with right hand) Thanks *Sin-No-More Spectacles!*

Announcer: Brought to you by King of Lies Industries and DEVIL Products, Inc.

Scripture reference: Matthew 5: 27-28 "You have heard that it was said, 'Do not commit adultery.' But I tell you that anyone who looks at a woman lustfully has already committed adultery with her in his heart."

5. CHRISTIANITY-MADE-EASY KIT (a commercial on a genuine walk with Christ)

Players:	Two; Announcer and Actor
Props:	A box
	A WWJD bracelet
	Fish car emblem
	Bumper sticker
	Fridge magnet
	Two book covers entitled "*How To Get The Most Out of Your Christian Friends*" and "*Proper Etiquette Around Christian Friends*".

Opening scene: As the announcer begins his monologue, the actor is seated in front of the audience acting thoughtful. The box of props is nearby but not in their hands.

CHRISTIANITY-MADE-EASY KIT

Announcer: Christians, Christians, Christians! They seem to be everywhere you look! In the newspapers, in politics, in hospitals, even the family next-door are Christians. Not only that, Christianity seems to be the popular thing to be right now with our Country's newfound "Spiritual Revival". But the lifestyle, it's so hard! You give up so much! What's a person to do? Fret no further friend. Pick up the phone and dial 1-800-C.O.S.T.U.M.E. for your *Christianity-Made-Easy Kit*.

(*The actor now picks up the box of props and displays them to the audience as the announcer introduces them.*)

Announcer: Inside you will be delighted to discover how easy being a Christian can be when you have all the right gear:

—A fish emblem for your minivan.

—A bumper sticker for your second car with a catchy Christian phrase.

—A WWJD bracelet in a fashion color of your choice.

—-And a fridge magnet with the popular Christian logo "*The Devil Put Calories Into Chocolate*".

But wait! If you order within the next ten minutes we will also include, at no extra cost, our two handy pocket guides entitled: "*Proper Etiquette Around Christian Friends*" and "*How to Get the Most Out of Your Christian Friends*". How can you lose? All this for just $19.95 plus access to the nicest people you'll ever want to take advantage of. Because Christianity is popular, eternal life is free for the taking, but the *Christianity-Made-Easy Kit* is nothing but money we're making!

Actor: (giving a "thumbs up sign" with right hand) Thanks *Christianity-Made-Easy Kit*!

Brought to you by King of Lies Industries and DEVIL Products, Inc.

Scripture reference: Matthew 6: 2-4 "So when you give to the needy, do not announce it with trumpets, as the hypocrites do in the synagogues and on the streets, to be honored by men. I tell you the truth, they have received their reward in full. But when you give to the needy, do not let your left hand know what your right hand is doing, so that your giving may be in secret. Then your father, who sees what is done in secret, will reward you."

6. THE ERASABLE BIBLE (a commercial on changing God's word).

Players:	One
Props:	A book with a cover that says "The Erasable Bible" and an eraser.

Opening scene: A single actor impersonating a crooked pastor is presenting the monologue.

THE ERASABLE BIBLE

Actor: No one likes to be disliked. At least I know I don't. I found this to be an issue in my life as I preached from God's word on Sundays in my church.

It seemed every Sunday after my sermons, I was bombarded by members of my flock who were offended in someway with how I presented God's word on topics such as the existence of Hell, or drunkenness or abortion and euthanasia. You know, the big issues, the ones everyone talks about in day-to-day life, at work around the water cooler.

I've found a way to elude these uncomfortable confrontations completely between myself and other members of my parish with this, (*actor displays the bible*) The Erasable Bible. The *Erasable Bible* is printed in a special type of ink that can be erased at my will, whenever and wherever the need arises.

It's lifted the burden of having to preach on the subjects that offend and concentrate more on the "feel good" topics like love, acceptance, thankfulness and non-judgmentality that are always so popular.

But what about the final passage of Revelation you say? Wait…let me see if I can quote it…"If anyone should add or delete any passage in this book…" Looks like a problem doesn't it? Not anymore. I'll just erase that too. (*Actor moves his eraser over his Bible like he is erasing the words*) See? Finally, the Bible and God's law and words of wisdom have come of age—now that's something I can live with.

Scripture reference: Revelation 22: 18-19 "I warn everyone who hears these words of the prophecy of this book: if anyone adds anything to them, God will add to him the plagues described in this book. And if anyone takes words away from this book of prophecy, God will take away from him his share in the tree of life and in the holy city, which are described in this book."

7. THE RUMOR RE-ROUTER TO FLATULENCE COLLAR (a commercial on changing bad habits, like gossiping)

Players:	Four; Announcer, and three teenage girls
Props:	Table with two sodas
	A ribbon or collar to put around player #3's neck.

Opening scene: Two girls sipping sodas at the mall, talking intensely to each other.

THE RUMOR RE-ROUTER TO FLATULANCE COLLAR

Announcer: Rumors. They are everywhere you go, destroying lives, causing suspicions, and decaying trust between the closest of friends and family. Why? Because gossip is fun, exciting, intriguing—in a word—it is SIN—and sin never claimed for a moment that it wasn't fun at times. So how can we stop the urge to gossip? How can we retrain our will to refrain from talking about others and their problems?

With the *Rumor Re-router to Flatulence Collar* that's how! Just like Pavlov's famous experiment where he conditioned a dog to salivate at the sound of a bell, a creature will learn a new habit with repeated exposure. The *"RRTFC"* will cure you of your urge to gossip by re-routing the sound of your voice from words of sin to embarrassing flatulent sounds every time the collar detects those destructive words coming out of your mouth. Just watch how the *"RRTFC"* can change your life.

(Two girls at the table with sodas)

Girl #1: Did you hear about Cliff and Tina?

Girl #2: Oh my gosh, do tell!

(Girl #3 enters wearing the collar)

Girl #1: Becky! Come sit. I've got an earful for you.

Girl #3: Wait, wait! Before you say anything, did you know that Andrea was caught pfffft! I mean that Andrea was pfffft pffft!

Girl #1: Gee Becky, I can't believe you did that in public!

Girl #2: Yeah, how embarrassing, maybe you need to spend some quality time in the ladies room…

Girl #3: No. Really pffft, pffft, pssssst. I've got to tell you pfffft!

Girl #1 Whoa girl! *(Fanning nose)*

(Looking around, Girl #3 runs off crying…)

Announcer: Through consistent exposure, the *"RRTFC"* will successfully train you to never gossip again!! Because walking the walk of a Christian is difficult, as well as talking the talk—we'll help you make sure you do it right.

Girl #3: (through tears) Thanks *Rumor Re-router to Flatulence Collar. (Sob!)*

Scripture reference: Proverbs 12: 18 "Reckless words pierce like a sword but the tongue of the wise brings healing."

8. THE HELL SUIT (a commercial on preparing for an uncertain life after death)

Players:	Two; Announcer and Actor
Props:	A snowsuit or coveralls stuffed with padding and covered in duct tape.

Opening scene: As the Announcer begins the monologue. The actor in the "Hell Suit" simply acts like a runway model.

THE HELL SUIT

Announcer: Are you confident of God's promise of forgiveness or are you someone who's come to terms with all of their sins, asked for forgiveness, given their heart to Jesus, but still feel uncertain as to where your soul will spend eternity? Perhaps instead, you're the type of person who is knee deep or deeper in past sin with way too much in your past or hidden in your closet to ever be fully cleansed. Heck, half the sins you've committed you've forgotten, lost track of, or even suppressed into the darkest reaches of your memory. There's no way you could confess them all. It would take years. And then again, maybe you're someone who's angry with the Almighty, unwilling to relent and too stubborn to admit your scandal. You're going to Hell and you ain't scared. If you could relate to any of these scenarios, then you're going to need a little after-life protection, a little, shall we say, eternal fire insurance?

You need *The Hell Suit*. The *Hell Suit* is a fully lined body suit made entirely out of asbestos, and comes complete with its own hose and coolant system. Nothing can beat the *Hell Suit*. It's going to get hot down there, and being buried in the *Hell Suit* will ensure that if you don't make it to heaven, then at least you'll have some protection in Hell. The *Hell Suit*: "The best use of asbestos ever invented"—says "Popular Mechanics", and they're right! We can all agree on the carcinogenic dangers of asbestos on living creatures, while asbestos on the dead makes the dead invincible. *The Hell Suit*—get caught dead in it.

Brought to you by King of Lies Industries and DEVIL Products, Inc.

Scripture reference: Revelation 20: 12-15 "And I saw the dead, great and small, standing before the throne, and books were opened. Another book was opened, which was the book of life. The dead were judged according to what they had done as recorded in the books. The sea gave up the dead that were in it, and death and Hades gave up the dead that were in them, and each person was judged according to what he had done. Then death and Hades were thrown into the lake of fire. The lake of fire was the second death. If anyone's name was not found written in the book of life, he was thrown into the lake of fire."

9. BAD IDEA JEANS (a commercial on making bad decisions)

Players:	Four; three regular guys and a breathy-voiced announcer
Props:	Pool cues or a basketball
	Three tags which say *"Bad Idea Jeans"* to tape to the back pocket of three of the player's jeans.

Opening scene: Four guys playing pool, all wearing jeans with "Bad Idea Jeans" logo on the back pocket.)

BAD IDEA JEANS

Guy #1: So, I figured, he has three cars and I only have one, he'll appreciate the fact that I've relieved him of that extra insurance payment.

Announcer: Bad Idea Jeans...

Guy #2: So she was looking at me, and I was looking at her, and one thing led to another and well, you know...

Announcer: Bad Idea Jeans...

Guy #3: Mom and Dad are so old and senile now; I've been able to swindle them out of just about everything they've owned...including my brother's inheritance.

Announcer: Bad Idea Jeans…

Guy #1: And then I noticed this guy stealing a lady's purse. I chased him down and beat the daylights out of him. I think he died.

Announcer: Bad Idea Jeans…

Guy #2: Well, I love golf so much that I constructed this giant shrine with my clubs and bag and every morning and evening I bow down to the shrine and ask it to bless my golf game and my life in general.

Announcer: Bad Idea Jeans…

Guy #4: So I got to thinking, I've got two lungs, and he only needs one new one to survive, so I offered up one of mine.

Guy #1: What? Are you crazy? That's the most insane thing I've ever heard.

Guy #2: Yeah! What kind of fool are you anyway?

(*Men continue to question Guy #4*)

Announcer: Bad Idea Jeans, when you're talking about sin, you're talking about a *bad idea*.

Brought to you by King of Lies Industries and DEVIL Products, Inc.

Scripture reference: Psalm 52: 1-2,5 "Why do you boast of evil, you mighty man? Why do you boast all day long you who are a disgrace in the eyes of God? Your tongue plots destruction; it's like a sharpened razor, you who practice deceit. Surely God will bring you down to everlasting ruin: He will snatch you up and tear you from your tent; He will uproot you from the land of the living."

10. THE FIVE FACES OF PURE JOY (a commercial on being joyful in troubled times)

Players:	Five; Person#1 (Jane), persons #2 & #3, Mom and the Announcer
Props:	Five large face photos from a magazine with lips cut out
	A "Y" shaped dental flossing tool.
	This commercial needs a little prep-work. You will need three large face photos from magazines that you

can cut out the mouth. The actor will hold the photo to their face and move their lips, making the photo look like it's talking. Also a "Y" shaped dental flossing tool is needed.

Opening scene: Two people talking—a third person runs up with bad news shortly after the announcer finishes his monologue.

THE FIVE FACES OF PURE JOY

Announcer: The Bible tells us to be happy, even joyful when faced with trouble or uncertainty. But who can really do it? What if you've just discovered you're going bankrupt, or that your spouse is moving out or even worse, that you have a terminal illness like cancer. People face these kinds of troubles every day and who knows who will be next, maybe you? And if it was you, how could you ever feel joyful or even crack a smile in times like these? God is really asking too much of his servants to be happy, or to praise him when it seems that he has abandoned them completely, but yet he tells us to do it. How will you do it? Do you have what it takes?

Now you do if you have the *Five Faces of Pure Joy*. You can go to church, work, or school with any of the *Five Faces of Pure Joy* and appear unscathed by the tragedy happening in your life. People will talk about what a strong Christian you are and that you exemplify what strength and faith should be. As a bonus gift, we'll include the *"Smile Exerciser"* so you can always have a back-up tool to carry off the facade of your joy in the event that you are without your *Five Faces of Pure Joy*. Watch how these necessary products can work for you."

Person #3: Jane, Jane! Your mother just called, and your father has just suffered a massive heart attack.

Person #1: Oh no! And I don't have any of my *"Five Faces"* with me. What am I going to do?

Person #2: Use the *Smile Exerciser!*

Person #1: Great idea! (*Person #3 takes out the flossing tool and raises the corners of her mouth into a smile with it*) We'll pick up one of my *Five Faces* on the way to the hospital.

Person #3: There's no use going to the hospital, Jane. Your father died before the ambulance got there.

Person #1: Oh well. I still feel joyful. (*She cries while pushing up edges of mouth into a smile with* Y *shaped flossing tool.*) I guess I better go see Mom; she may need one of the "*Five Faces.*"

Announcer: Has anything like this ever happened to you? If it hasn't, we can guarantee that it's all just a matter of time until it does. And how will you maintain your joy facade in front of your Christian friends?

(*Person #1 approaches Mom who's crying into a hanky. Person #1 is already wearing a face—lips poking through the photo where the lips should be.*)

Person #1: Hi Mom. I thought you could use one of these.

Mom: Thank you dear. How right you are. (*She puts on the face.*) There that's better. I'm really happy that Dad is on his way to heaven. I don't even feel a bit lonely. Now I'll have more time to spend with my girlfriends at Bridge Club.

Person #1: Yes! And Christmas will be a little less expensive, with one person less to buy for.

(*Both ladies fight tears*)

Person #1: Aren't we being so good at being obedient to God?

(*Mother nods*)

Announcer: Buy the *Five Faces of Pure Joy* now because you never know when trouble will knock you down.

Person #1 and Mom: (*giving a "thumbs up sign" with their right hands*) Thanks FFPJ!

Announcer: Brought to you by King of Lies Industries and DEVIL Products, Inc.

Scripture reference: James 1: 2-4 "Consider it pure joy my brothers, whenever you face trials of many kinds, because you know that the testing of your faith develops perseverance. Perseverance must finish its work so that you may be mature and complete, not lacking anything."

Isaiah 41: 10 "So do not fear for I am with you; do not be dismayed for I am your God. I will strengthen you and help you; I will uphold you with my righteous right hand."

DISCUSSION STARTERS

There is a Biblical message involved in each one of "Matt's Mental Moments" and "Tiffany's Epiphanies" but they are presented as the inner thoughts of the actors themselves and are purposefully left without a conclusion. To set the scene, I suggest a single actor sitting thoughtfully with a diary, saying nothing but acting like they are thinking deeply about the topic at hand, which is being read out loud by another actor who is off stage. Another way to present these discussion starters is to copy them onto transparency sheets, and put them on an overhead projector. Then, an actor can read the words out loud from either off or on stage. In both cases, it is a great effect to include soft instrumental music in the background.

1. Matt's Mental Moment #1 (deep thoughts on lasting satisfaction)

I wonder if it's possible for a person to see everything that there is to see in the world, like people places and things, and ever be bored. Is it possible for that person to be disappointed when presented with a map of the whole world by a travel agent and asked "where to?" Only to reply, "is this all there is?"

I guess that in the world that we live in, it's hard to be satisfied with what we have or what we've experienced. Every television and magazine I've seen encourages me to buy more, see more, experience more. In striving to do all those things, would I ever feel like I'd seen, bought, and experienced enough or would I always be driven to top the last thing I had just done?

Matthew 6:33 says "Seek first the kingdom of God, and all his righteousness, and all these things will be added unto you."

All things. Does that mean that if I put God first in my life, He will reward me with material goods? He blessed both David and Solomon in that way.

Or does that mean that true heart felt satisfaction concerning all the aspects of your life comes from living for God, and as a result, the desire you once had for all the other things just fades away?

I wonder…

2. Matt's Mental Moment #2 (deep thoughts on being a servant of God)

Matthew 20:77 says "Whoever desires to be first among you, let him be your slave."

And it's got me thinking. I'd like to be thought of as "first." As a matter of fact, I'd like to be well liked and respected by all of my peers, and who wouldn't? With that kind of respect comes…power.

But if to be first, I must be a slave to everyone, does that mean that I would have to carry everyone's books, do their homework, clean their garage, and even mow their lawns to gain their respect?

Leaders in history like Stalin, Saddam Hussein, and Hitler gained their power by simply demanding it of their people. The ones who refused to bow down to them were publicly murdered to serve as an example to others to respect their power.

I'll bet that none of those men ever had to mow a lawn or clean a garage.

But that's not the kind of leader I'd want to be.

Killing people just isn't my bag.

Jesus' story shows a man who always put the needs of others before his own. And while the afore-mentioned leaders are only remembered in history books, Jesus is the most famous and powerful leader to ever walk the planet. Not a day goes by that his teachings or his people come up in the news and it's been over 2000 years since he lived in the flesh.

Jesus' leadership style was radically different than anyone else. It was one of humility and unselfish service to others. He even went so far as to willingly allow his own murder at the age of thirty-three so that even the men who killed him might have an opportunity to have everlasting life.

Rather than forcing servant ship from his people, He showed that He too was a servant of God, doing his duty on earth by being kind, loving, and giving to others.

So, maybe forcing your power over other people isn't the trait of a lasting leader. It's more about serving their needs that gains you their respect.

Hmmmmmmmm…

3. Matt's Mental Moment's #3 (deep thoughts on God's attitude regarding our prayers)

I wonder if God is ever unconvinced by my prayers. I wonder if he ever gets frustrated with how, I begin to pray at night, but fall asleep long before I ever say "Amen."

When I ask God for his help, like on an exam or to play well in a basketball game, I wonder if he even considers my requests when there are so many other people in the world who are facing much bigger problems.

Luke 11:9 says "Ask and it will be given to you."

Does that mean that I can ask for anything and God will grant my requests like a genie in a lamp would do?

Or, does it all depend on the motivation behind the request.

It always seems like there's a catch.

If I'm asking for help to ace a math exam because I haven't studied and I need a miracle to pass the class, will God provide that miracle even when I don't deserve it? Would it be more likely that God would instead grant me a good night sleep, a clear head and a calm spirit going into the exam as an answer to my request after I've studied hard, and truly deserve the grade.

God may never tire of my requests, but I guess to Him the answering belongs. My part would simply be in the asking, but more importantly asking when I know that my request is for reasons beyond laziness or selfishness.

Hmmmmmmm…

4. Matt's Mental Moment's #4 (deep thoughts on right thinking and right living)

The Bible gives clear guidelines on the kinds of things we should think about. Philippians 4: 8 state's that: "if there is any virtue and if there is anything praiseworthy-meditate on these things."

Psalm 1: 2 and Psalm 119:57 say to meditate on God's word day and night, that it should be first priority.

But how am I supposed to think about God's word all day and night when I have a life to live?

I remember Paul saying that we are to think upon things that are true, noble, just, pure, lovely, of good report, virtuous and praiseworthy, and allow those things to govern our minds.

Does this mean that keeping all these good things on your mind, day to day, minute to minute while you are living your life, make you into a good person?

Can evil thoughts, placed in your mind by television, movies, other people and situations affect your heart enough to make you a bad person?

I wonder.

5. Matt's Mental Moment's #5 (deep thoughts on prejudice)

If I notice a person who seems a little different, someone that nobody else is talking to, am I being prejudiced by not approaching and talking to them?

James 2:1 says, "Do not hold the faith of our Lord Jesus Christ, the Lord of Glory with partiality."

If this is true, then when I am showing favoritism, I'm sinning against people whom God loves and for whom Christ died.

If I cling to my usual group of friends while I'm at Church and ignore the people who don't seem to belong to a group of friends, people who seem to be left out, then am I saying that those people aren't good enough to be accepted by my God?

When I ignore people who need acceptance in church, am I being a hypocrite?

I wonder...

6. Tiffany's Epiphanies #1 (deep thoughts on breaking your routine)

My devotional time with God has been dry.

Dry as the desert.

And consequently, so has been my spirit.

I'm distracted, discontented, and disconnected.

It seems like there are so many other big issues encompassing my life everyday that I have little time to dedicate to God, let alone, listen for his answers.

I'm busy.

Busy with school, busy with friends and relationships. Busy with everything that isn't about God and somehow the clear connection that I once felt with God is now full of static.

Matthew 14: 23 talks about how Jesus would go up on the mountain to be alone when he wanted to pray. I guess that even the Son of God had times where he felt like he needed to reconnect with the Father.

Hmmm…Jesus went to the top of a mountain to escape the crowds and the distraction around him so that he could hear God.

If I were to change my routine a bit, take my Bible somewhere lovely like, under a big shade tree or to the beach or even out into my backyard where I could escape from all of my busyness, would my spirit reconnect with God?

I wonder…

7. Tiffany's Epiphanies #2 (deep thoughts on gossip)

If everyone were to stop their gossiping, would anyone have anything to say?

I know that gossiping is wrong but why is it so intriguing, even…fun at times? The only time that gossip isn't fun is when the talk is centered on my family or myself. Like the time a rumor was being spread throughout the people in my church that my parents were getting a divorce. The rumor wasn't true, but just knowing that everyone had been talking about it made me feel uncomfortable around people that I had trusted. I even noticed that the people who I thought cared about my family began to treat us differently, and that hurt.

As a result of the rumor, my family left the congregation of that church and although my brother and I found new church homes, our parents have never been back to any church since.

James 4: 11 says, "Do not speak evil of one another."

If I repeat a rumor to another person, therefore fueling its destructive power, have I spoken with an evil tongue? Even more, have I allowed Satan to use me to hurt someone, like how my parents were hurt by their church friends?

I wonder…

8. Tiffany's Epiphanies #3 (deep thoughts on exaggeration)

Have you ever noticed how a small canker sore to your cheek or tongue can look so little but feel enormous in your mouth?

James 3:5 says "The tongue is a little member who boasts big things."

So, the tongue is an exaggerator both physically and verbally.

I find that when I'm telling a story about something that has happened to me, I have a habit of exaggerating the details and do it without even trying. A molehill of an experience quickly turns into a mountain of action and drama as I stretch the truth beyond its boundaries.

The fun part about this is that everyone seems to love my stories.

What bothers me however is that over time I've noticed how this innocent tendency I have to exaggerate has damaged my testimony. People are suspecting that what I have to say isn't true, even before I finish saying it.

And if what I'm saying really weren't true, then that would make it, a lie? Does my habit of compulsive exaggeration make me a compulsive liar?

I wonder…

9. Tiffany's Epiphanies #4 (deep thoughts on unanswered questions)

If I could talk to God face to face, in human form, there would be so many questions that I'd have.

What was the point in creating mosquitoes?

Where do dinosaurs fit into creationism?

What will it feel like when my body dies and my spirit ascends to you?

Is eternity in Heaven without chores? Once you get there, is it all about play?

Do human spirits receive missions as guardian angels who are then sent back to earth to help people who are still spiritually lost?

I could go on. It's hard not to know the answers to these questions. It's even harder not to let these unanswered questions affect my faith.

1 Timothy 1:15 says "This is a faithful saying, and worthy of all acceptance, that Christ Jesus came into the world to save sinners, of whom I am chief."

When I feel overwhelmed and challenged by the questions that can't be explained by science, I try to remember that Jesus came to save our souls, not to satisfy our curiosity.

Besides, where would the challenge be in having faith if everything that challenges us to believe without seeing was scientifically explainable?

10. Tiffany's Epiphanies #5 (deep thoughts on having a basis for your moral opinion)

If a person says, "I don't believe in God," it makes me wonder if that person can say they believe that there is a difference between right and wrong.

Even before our country was founded, actions that were considered "right" verses actions that were considered "wrong" and "punishable," were defined by what the Bible listed in the Ten Commandments.

"Thou shalt not murder" is a good example of a law that is widely accepted all over the world with extreme consequences attached. If a person doesn't believe in God, how can they also say "I believe murder is wrong." The Ten Commandments were given to us as a guide on how to live happier lives. If you don't believe in God, why would you even care if murder were right or wrong? If you don't believe that there is a Heaven and a Hell, why would it matter to you if you or anyone else stole, murdered, coveted, cheated and all the rest? If you're living only for yourself, with no incentive of a heavenly place to spend your eternity, what's to keep you from creating your own laws? Furthermore, what's to keep you from doing whatever it takes to make your one life on earth the most profitable and comfortable life it can be even at the expense of others?

I wonder…

SKITS

What do you get when you take a room full of people who love to have fun and present to them a bouquet of colorful characters in a multitude of diverse situations? You get the best that "Silly Salad" has to offer delivered to you in voracious laughter.

1. FOUR FACES (a silly, musical skit)

Players: Four

Props: A large piece of cardboard with four holes cut in it, just large enough for four actors to put their faces in.

Opening scene: The four actors place their faces in the open holes of the piece of cardboard, facing the audience. Each face maintains a specific expression throughout the skit. Example:

Face 1—is scared, concerned, shifty eyed.

Face 2—is happy, joyful, elated.

Face 3—is angry, glaring.

Face 4—is sad, crying, sobbing, mournful.

Any song or play on words will work for this skit, try any of these well-known songs, having the four faces sing them while maintaining their designated mood.

Songs: 1. "Who Did Swallow Jonah Down?"

2. "Joy, Joy, Joy, Joy, Down in My Heart."

3. "Saints Go Marching In."

4. "Another One Bites The Dust."

5. "Old Mc Donald"

2. CHIN BAND (another silly musical skit)

Players:	Two—Four
Props:	Eye make-up
	Lipstick
	Pillows
	Blankets

Opening scene: Players lay down with the top of their heads toward the audience. Propping pillows under their necks will therefore raise their chins up into the air. Then, they are to cover their faces from the nose to the forehead with a blanket. On the tip of their chins two eyes and a nose, lipstick should be applied to their lips. Little hats or tufts of hair can be placed on the end of the chin for a more realistic effect.

The chin band can then sing or do a rhythmic piece using their mouths.

Example:	Chin 1 says: "Bob, bob, bob, etc."
	Chin 2 says: "Boom, chica, chica, chica, boom, etc."
	Chin 3 says: "Shwee, shwee, dum, bum, shwee, shwee, etc."
	Chin 4 says: "Oh baby, baby, oh baby, baby, etc."

The chin band can also take requests from the audience.

3. GRUMPY OLD GRANNIES (a skit on God's consistency through the ages.)

Players:	Two; Marjorie and Phyllis
Props:	Hair rollers
	Nightgowns and slippers
	Wheel chairs or canes

Character analysis: Both these crabby old gals have had their share of living. The young folks don't know how good they've got it and they feel it's their duty to tell them so.

Opening scene: Marjorie is already seated in her rocking chair while Phyllis enters to take a seat next to her.

GRUMPY OLD GRANNIES

Phyllis: G'morning Marjorie, how's it going?

Marjorie: "Well, if it weren't for the fact that I passed a gallstone the size of a tangerine this morning, then I'd say I was doing alright.

Phyllis: I hear you, I mean when we were young, we didn't have tangerines, all we had were heads of cabbage and that's how we got our vitamin C and we didn't complain one bit about it.

Marjorie: That's right, we liked it!

Phyllis: We loved it!

Marjorie: Yes, we loved it. And vitamins, we didn't have Flintstones or Rug rats vitamins, we ate copper wire and nails for our minerals and got our calcium from the bones of cow carcasses we'd find on the prairie and we didn't fuss.

Phyllis: That's right, we liked it.

Marjorie: We loved it.

Phyllis: Yes indeed-eee-do, and when we were young we didn't have cartoons. We'd pick the fleas off of the dogs and make them race each other and then the owner of the winning flea would get a treat.

Marjorie: Right, that was our entertainment and we liked it.

Phyllis: We loved it.

Marjorie: Yes, we loved it and we didn't have treats like the kids do these days. We didn't have sodee pop, Nerds, or Chic-o-sticks. Heck, we didn't even have Popsicles.

Phyllis: That's right. We'd pour our Kool-Aid out on flat rocks and let it freeze over night then we'd get up early before the sun got too warm and lick the rocks. We didn't complain. We liked it. We loved it, in fact.

Marjorie: That's right, and once October came and all us kids were expected to dress up and go trick or treating, we didn't have any Power Rangers or JarJar Binks costumes. No, we used what we had around the house, like a plant or a spoon and we'd go door-to-door saying, "Look at me, I'm Super Spoon Head Woman" or "I'm Captain Green Thumb, trick-or-treat!"

Phyllis: And we were thankful for those plants and spoons. At least we know that there is one thing that will never change, right Marjorie?

Marjorie: Right. Wednesday's are always meatloaf…

Phyllis: No, no, you senile old hoolie dog. It's God. He's never going to change. He's the same yesterday, today, and forever.

Marjorie: I say Amen to that!

Scripture reference: Hebrews 13: 7-8 "Remember your leaders who spoke the word of God to you. Consider the outcome of their way of life and imitate their faith. Jesus Christ is the same yesterday and today and forever."

4. SYD FROST ON JACOB

Players:	Two (Syd and his breathy counterpart who says the lines in *italic print*.)
Props:	Costume for Syd: Dark glasses, black beret, black turtleneck shirt, black pants and shoes.

Character analysis: Syd Frost is a beatnik poet; he is very cool and very serious about his work. Use dramatic pauses and rhythmic background sounds i.e.: bongo drums, triangle, and cymbals to create the mood of Syd's poetic reading.

Opening scene: Syd sits center stage on a stool.

SYD FROST ON JACOB

Syd Frost: Jacob had twelve sons,

Joseph was his favorite one.

He gave Jo a robe of colors,

Which made the others crazy jealous.

One night by moonlight Jo told his bro's

I've had a dream, someday I will be king!

The brothers got angry and plotted an evil thing.

> *(What'd they do Syd?)*

They dug a pit and threw him in.

> *(ou!)*

And pondered over killing him.

> *(Oh, No)*

Instead they stole his coat, so handsome, and sold him to Egyptians for a hefty ransom

At home they told their father he'd died, killed by a wild animal, eaten alive.

> *(No!)*

For weeks Dad cried

> *(How sad, Syd)*

But don't despair of this story my friend,

As you will discover the work of God's hand.

Once in Egypt he was thrown in prison for life,

For refusing the advances of Potiphar's wife.

But even in prison, God was with him.

> *(Tell us Syd)*

Down in the dungeon where mice and rats played,

An imprisoned butler of the Pharaoh dismayed.

"I've had a strange dream" and he shared with Jo Jo that day, and Joseph explained.

You will have your old job back in exactly three days.

(Did it happen?)

Affirmative

(Way to go Jo)

You see God had given our JoJo a power to interpret dreams that would foretell the future!

It wasn't too long before the Pharaoh did summon Joseph to his palace to discuss a dream that quite bugged him.

(Uh Huh!)

There are seven fat cows and seven thin cows all coming out of the river.

The seven thin cows ate the seven fat cows and were still as thin as silver.

(Weird)

"God has told you of His plan!" Jo said to the powerful man.

The seven fat cows are the years of plenty. The seven thin cows are famine across the land

The Pharaoh was so grateful to Jo and his gift of interpretation,

He soon made him ruler of the Egyptian nation.

(Did the dream come true?)

Of course

(Uh huh!)

When the famine did come and Egypt should of died of starvation, Jo had prepared and stored food for his nation.

It would seem all was lost for others who lived off the land.

Remember the brothers who sold Jo for some silver?

(Uh huh)

They came into Egypt to seek help from the new king. Little did they know, he was their long lost sibling.

> *(Did he have them killed Syd?)*

No.

> *(How' bout put in prison?)*

No.

It was true they deserved it, but that's not the way Jo would go

> *(What'd he do?)*

He reached out with his arms and smiled a grand smile,

Then said, "My brothers, it's sure been awhile."

> *(Did he send them back hungry? I'll bet his riches he flaunted)*

No, he opened his kingdom and gave them all that they wanted.

Scripture reference for discussion: The story of Jacob and his brothers is found in the book of Genesis chapters thirty-seven through forty-seven.

5. SYD FROST ON MOSES

Players:	Two (Syd and his breathy counterpart who says the lines in italic *print*.)
Props:	Costume for Syd: Dark glasses, black beret, black turtleneck shirt, black pants and shoes.

Character analysis: Syd Frost is a beatnik poet; he is very cool and very serious about his work. Use dramatic pauses and rhythmic background sounds, i.e.: bongo drums, triangle, and cymbals to set the mood of Syd's poetic reading.

Opening scene: Syd appears center stage on a stool.

SYD FROST ON MOSES

Let me tell you a story 'bout some cats I know who lived in Egypt Land.
The Pharaoh had taken control of all their things,
Had those people in the palm of his evil hand.

But there were these people called the Israelites,
Who didn't want to play his game.
So the Pharaoh forced those people into slavery,
Causing them grief and shame.

Well, the Lord in heaven was sad to see His people and their pain.
So he called out a cat from Midian.
Moses was his name.

Moses was afraid to do the work of God or of a single word to utter.
"Lord," he asked with his heart in his throat, "don't you remember that I
S-s-s-stutter?"
God said,

      GO DOWN   MOSES
          (GO DOWN   MOSES)
      GO DOWN   TO EGYPT LAND
          (WAY DOWN)

Well, Moses he obeyed and went to the Pharaoh,
Approached him at his throne.
He said, "If you don't comply, all the first born Egyptians will die,
So...let my people go."

(Let my people go)

Pharaoh let them go but not until after he'd suffered from different
plagues on his nation.
When Mo's escape plan erupted,
Pharaoh's heart corrupted as a result of his excessive frustration.

      GO DOWN   MOSES
         (GO DOWN)   *(MOSES)*
      GO DOWN   TO EGYPT LAND
         (WAY DOWN)   *(TO EGYPT LAND)*

And here is the message,
The Lord did grant safe passage to Mo's people through the bottom of the
sea.

Pharaoh's army died frightened as the water collided and
God's ultimate power was seen.

But what I want you to hear friends, is to have no fear;
When the Lord calls you to do a good deed, He will protect you,
No Pharaoh will wreck you, his power will set people *FREE.*

(Preach it, Syd)

*Scripture reference for discussion: The story of Moses and his mission to deliver the
Israelites out of the hands of the evil pharaoh is found in the book of Exodus
Chapters Two through Fourteen.*

6. MORALS OVER COFFEE WITH DR. MEREDITH STEIN SHOW, Episode one: naughty girls of the Bible

Players:	Six; Meredith, Bath Sheba, Jezebel, two callers, and an announcer
Props:	Dr. Meredith's costume—make it outrageous
	Bath Sheba's outfit—make it pretty
	Jezebel's outfit—make it naughty
	Three coffee mugs, sofa, coffee table
	Map of the US on poster board with the logo "Spankings across America" on it
	Star stickers

Character analysis: Meredith is a self proclaimed "Moralologist" with a New Jersey accent and a strong belief in capital punishment. She's boisterous, intrusive and intimidating. She could also be your best friend, that is, if you live your life right.

Opening scene: While the announcer introduces Dr. Meredith, she sits on her sofa drinking her coffee looking confident.

MORALS OVER COFFEE WITH DR. MEREDITH STEIN SHOW Episode one

Announcer: It's time for the Morals Over Coffee With Dr. Meredith Stein Show! The show where moral issues are discussed and debated with "Moralologist" and disciplinary enthusiast, Dr. Meredith Stein!

(Applause, spotlight on Dr. Meredith set)

Dr. Stein: Thank you, welcome to Morals over Coffee with Dr. Meredith Stein. I'm Dr. Meredith. Tonight on the show we will be discussing moral issues with some famous naughty girls of the Old Testament. We'll get their side of the story, and maybe let them try and justify their actions, whether they are moral or immoral. After all, who are we to judge? Let's welcome King David's famous mistress, Bath Sheba.

(Applause, Dr Meredith stands and hands Bath Sheba a cup of coffee—she sits)

Dr. Stein: Welcome to the show.

Bath Sheba: I'm very happy to be here.

Dr. Stein: Now, Bath Sheba, some of our viewers know your story as it is told in 2 Samuel, Chapter 11, but not everyone is familiar with it. What the nation wants to know is why you thought you had to be in the buff while you were in plain sight of the King's window. Were you just trying to avoid tan lines or what? Could you give us a brief synopsis?

Bath Sheba: Yes. Well, I was up there taking a bath, enjoying the sunshine and King David just happened to see me. He must have liked what I had to offer because he summoned me to his palace were one thing led to another and before I knew it, I was pregnant with his child.

Dr. Stein: Are you saying you were trying to seduce him the whole time?

Bath Sheba: Of course, after all he is the King…

Dr. Stein: I can't let this conversation go on any further, it's time to give you a moral spanking!

(*Dr. Meredith bends Bath Sheba over her knee and spanks her, she leaves in disgust*)

Dr. Stein: It's time to take a call, this is Wanda from Tennessee. Hello Wanda, you're on Morals over Coffee with Dr. Meredith Stein. What's your moral issue?

Caller: Yes, I'm very nervous. Thanks for taking my call. I don't want you to get mad, but I must say that I disagree with how you treated that young lady. You didn't witness to her about forgiveness or repentance…

Dr. Stein: Wait Wanda, "wimpy Wanda from Tenneseenie-I'm-a-weenie," what you need is a good spanking. Mr. Farley! Get her address and send someone over to spank her soundly…you know you've got a bleeding heart, on the line when they feel like they have to stick up for Bath Sheba. Let's put a star on our chart in the state of Tennessee.

(*Meredith places a star sticker on the state of Tennessee as seen on her "Morals across America" map.*)

Announcer: All right, we have time for one more guest please. Welcome, from the book of 2 Kings, Chapter 9, Jezebel.

(*Jezebel enters, Meredith stands and offers her coffee, they both sit*)

Dr. Stein: Welcome, Jezebel.

Jezebel: I just saw Bath Sheba running out of here crying. What's her deal?

Dr. Stein: Oh, she'll be fine, that is until she dies and then she'll really be in for it. Anyway, Jezzie, you have a certain reputation for being somewhat evil. Do you have anything to say about that?

Jezebel: I'm just a regular girl, trying to make my way in the world. I simply arranged the murders of several powerful people to secure my career.

(*Dr. Meredith falls to the floor feigning a heart attack, clutching her left arm*)

Dr. Stein: It appears that you are lacking in any kind of remorse.

Jezebel: Why should I feel bad? Isn't life all about getting what you want?

Dr. Stein: I can't bear to let this conversation go on any further. It's time for your moral spanking!

(*Meredith bends Jezebel over her knee and spanks her, Jezebel leaves in disgust*)

Dr. Stein: You'd better run! From what I hear, God's got it in for you!

Announcer: That's all for our show, I hope you've enjoyed Morals Over Coffee. Goodnight!

(*Applause*)

Scripture reference for discussion: *The story of Bath Sheba and her relationship with King David is found in the book of 2 Samuel Chapter Eleven. For Jezebel's story, read 1 Kings Chapter Nine.*

7. MORALS OVER COFFEE WITH Dr. MEREDITH STEIN SHOW Episode two: Disobedience and its Consequences

Players:	Five; Meredith, Lot's wife, Jonah, Sharon, and an announcer
Props:	Dr. Meredith's costume—make it outrageous.
	Lot's wife's costume—make it white and sparkly, with a fake finger
	Jonah's costume—make it prophet-like
	Two coffee cups, bowl of popcorn, coffee grinder, coffee table and sofa
	Map of the US on poster board with the logo "Spankings across America" on it
	Star stickers
	Something to wheel in Lot's wife, like a dolly or a child's wagon

Character analysis: Meredith is a self proclaimed "Moralologist" with a New Jersey accent and a strong believer in capital punishment. She's boisterous, intrusive and intimidating. She could also be your best friend, that is, if you live your life right.

Opening scene: While the announcer introduces Dr. Meredith, she sits on her sofa drinking her coffee and looking confident.

MORALS OVER COFFEE WITH DR. MEREDITH STEIN SHOW Episode two

Announcer: It's time once again for the Morals Over Coffee With Dr. Meredith Stein Show, the show where moral issues are discussed and debated with "Moralologist" and disciplinary enthusiast, Dr. Meredith Stein!

(Applause, spotlight on Dr. Meredith)

Dr. Stein: Thank you, welcome once again to the Morals Over Coffee with Dr. Meredith Stein. I'm Dr. Meredith. Tonight we will be discussing, over coffee and a little popcorn, the issue of disobedience to God and it's consequences. We have some interesting guests lined up for tonight's show. We'll talk over coffee with them, get their side of the story, and let them try to justify their behavior whether it is moral or immoral. After all, we are not to judge. Let's welcome, from the book of Genesis, the woman who stands out as a pillar of disobedience—Lot's Wife.

(Applause as Lot's wife is wheeled out on a dolly—she is all white, sparkly and stiff in a "looking behind herself" position.)

Dr. Stein: Well, it appears that you are in much the same condition that you were when we last heard about you. Now, let's see, your husband told you that God's angels told him to tell you not to look back, but you couldn't help yourself, could you? Saving your life wasn't enough. You had to see the fire and brimstone coming down on Sodom and Gomorrah. You just couldn't obey. Well, what do you have to say about it? Do you have any advice for our viewers?

Lot's Wife: (*talks without moving lips—in a muffled voice.*) Don't disobey God…it's not worth it.

Dr. Stein: Thanks; we'll take it from someone who knows.

(As Lot's wife is being wheeled off stage, Dr. Stein breaks a finger off of Lot's wife and pops it into a grinder—then salts popcorn with it.)

Dr. Stein: All right, on with the show. Next up we'll talk to Jonah, let's welcome him shall we?

(Applause, Jonah appears looking disheveled)

Dr. Stein: Welcome Jonah, coffee?

Jonah: No, thanks.

Dr. Stein: Popcorn?

Jonah: Yes, thank-you.

(Jonah helps himself to some popcorn)

Dr. Stein: So, what gives Jonah? The word is you were swallowed up by a whale, God allowed you to live and so on but even after his display of mercy, you still didn't understand what God was trying to teach you is this right?

Jonah: Well, that all depends on whom you're talking to. If your talking to God, the one who instrumented the whole deal then that would be correct. However, if you are speaking to me, Jonah—the one who had to actually go through it then the subject is debatable. I mean God knew, He *knew* I hated the people of Nineveh, that my family had a history of bad blood with them and *still* He made me go. By intimidating me by sending the fish to swallow me; then causing the tree, which grew to provide shade for me, to suddenly wither and die. He's just got it out for me. He doesn't show *me* any respect. He could have asked any…

(Meredith begins to feign a heart attack and gasps for breath. Pounding her chest to restart her heart—self-CPR)

Jonah: (continues *however is distracted by Dr. Meredith's behavior*)…of his prophets or priests to go talk to those dogs of Nineveh, those insolent slobs!

Dr. Stein: Stop! Stop! I can't stand the blasphemy! You're killing me! What you need is a moral spanking—something to whale that pride right out of you—old' boy! And it's been a long time in coming!

(Meredith turns Jonah over her knee and spanks him)

Dr. Stein (continued): Now get outta here—and I wouldn't advise going swimming until you change your attitude. Let's take a call. This is Sharon from Friendswood, California. Yes, Sharon, you're on the Morals Over Coffee With Dr. Meredith Stein—what's on your mind?

Sharon: Dr. Meredith, I've been listening to your show and I am appalled at how you have chosen to portray our Heavenly Father as a mean, easily angered, abusive God—He's not that way at all, He is a God of love—

Dr. Stein: Alright, hold it Sharon, Sharon from California, "watch me call in and bore ya" I've got endless examples let's see…Sapphira and her husband Ananias in Acts 5: 1-11, who just dropped dead after it's revealed they tried to deceive God. All the people in Sodom and Gomorrah. All the living creatures; except Noah and his family in Genesis. Uzzah, the highest priest of the Levite covenant who touched the Ark—which was a no, no and died instantly. Moses & Aaron who didn't get to go to the Promised Land from disobedience. Saul, who was not to leave any Philistines alive or to take anything, lost his kingdom.

Sharon: But that's all Old Testament stuff. Once Jesus came everything changed!

Dr. Stein: Mr. Farley, that poor woman has never been disciplined properly. Don't worry, Sharon, help is on the way. Mr. Farley will be there as soon as possible to give you the moral spanking you need. A sound spanking will cleanse you of your wimpiness. Let's put a star on the chart of our Morals Across America Campaign.

(Dr. Meredith places a star sticker on the state of California)

Dr. Meredith: Taking it one spanking at a time but making a difference in this great country of ours. Until we meet again America. Goodnight!

Scripture reference for discussion: The story of the destruction of Sodom and Gomorrah followed by the fate of Lot's wife is found in the book of Genesis, Chapter Nineteen.

Romans 5: 19-21 "For just as through the disobedience of the one man the many were made sinners, so also through the disobedience of the one man the many will be made righteous. The law was added so that the trespass might increase. But where sin increased, grace increased all the more, so that, just as sin reigned in death, so also grace might reign through righteousness to bring eternal life through Jesus Christ our Lord."

Romans 11: 30–32 *"Just as you who were at one time disobedient to God have now received mercy as a result of their disobedience, so they too have now become disobedient to receive mercy as a result of God's mercy to you. For God has bound all men over to disobedience so that he may have mercy on them all."*

8. GUT GETASTEN WITH HELGA AND INGA WEISBERG Episode one (a skit on how life's not always fair)

"Gut Getasten" is pronounced: goot ge-taste-in.

Players:	Four; Helga, Inga, announcer, and a studio guest
Props:	Helga & Inga's costumes—make them German looking
	A table with the following items on it: kitchen tools, bowls, seasonings, one cookie, two steins with hot cocoa, and canned whip cream.

Character analysis: Helga and Inga are two very jolly sisters from Germany who host their own cooking show. They do more talking than cooking and in the end, help to solve the problems of the studio guest. They are very close, rarely argue with each other and can tell tall tales about their homeland. Have fun with these two, the sillier the better and a German accent is imperative.

*Beer stein dance routine: The beer stein dance routine is were Helga and Inga bump their steins together, take a drink, bump their bottoms together then shout "Ja!" simultaneously.

Opening Scene: Helga and Inga are at the table mixing the pretend contents of their bowls. Two giant beer steins filled with hot cocoa as well as a can of canned whipped cream are on the table as well.

GUT GETASTEN WITH HELGA & INGA WEISSBERG
Episode one

Announcer: And now it's time for everybody's favorite cooking encouragement duo, Helga and Inga!

(Applause)

Helga: Welkommen, Gutentag. Welcome to Gut Getasten with Helga and Inga, I am Helga.

Inga: Unt I am Inga!

Helga: Ja, unt we hope to put a little spice in your life with our original recipes from the heart.

Inga: Zat is right Helga. Unt alzo through the help of our studio audience and our good Lord, we all may learn a thing or two about how to live our lives better in dis world.

Helga: So without any further delay, let's bring out today's guest Miss_____.

(Applause)

Helga & Inga: Welcome, Miss_____.

Miss_____: Thank you, I'm happy to be here.

Helga: It's good to see you. How is everything going in your teenage life?

Miss_____: Oh fine, just fine.

(Helga and Inga look at each other)

Helga and Inga: Really?

Miss_____: Yes, really, I'm just…great.

Inga: Why don't you cut the verspotten and tell us the truth?

Helga: Ja, we were teens once too, unt we know a pouty teen when we see one.

Miss_____: Well, there's this dance this weekend and my mom said I couldn't go. It's just not fair! My brother got to go to dances at my age and all my friends will be there—I'll be the only one missing. It's going to ruin my reputation; it's just not fair.

(Helga and Inga discuss heatedly in German between themselves, then do special*beer stein dance routine.)

Helga: Ja!

Inga: Good hot cocoa!

Helga: Okay, first, life is not fair. Inga and I have a very difficult story to share with you that will reopen old wounds of our childhood, but we want to help.

Inga: Ja, it begins at an old farm, where we used to live as children and where we had a pet piggy.

Helga: Named him Ferkel, unt we loved him so much, dressed him in dolly clothes and carried him in the baskets of our bikes. And when he got big we dressed like the Cowgirls of the West and rode Ferkel about the farm.

Inga: Zen one day, little Ferkel disappeared. For weeks we looked for him all about the barnyard, pouted and cried and nearly drove our poor Mutter to craziness!

Helga: Finally, one night at the supper table she could take no more and when Inga asked for the millionth time, "Where ist Ferkel?" Mutter spat out "Ferkel ist that steaming giant Bratwurst on your plate dare. Now gobble every bite or there will be no apple strudel for dessert!"

Miss_____: *(pauses in shock)* I'm sure your mother understood how much Ferkel meant to you when you refused to eat and skipped dessert.

(Helga and Inga look at each other)

Inga: Skip dessert?

Helga: We ate the Bratwurst it was delicious!

Inga: But you are missing the point, Mutter wasn't trying to be mean, she was doing what was best for us by putting food on our table just like your Mutter is just trying to keep you safe. And like with Ferkel, life just always isn't fair.

Helga: Ja, so quit being such a gepoopstink and go home and love your Mutter. Bless her heart.

Miss_____: But…

Inga: I know something that will help ease this emotional teenage pain.

Helga: Ah, yes.

Inga: A little Lieb Kuchen! (*Inga hands the guest a cookie*) Bye, bye!

Helga: Problem solved! Let's dance!

(*Helga and Inga do the*beer stein routine*)

Helga & Inga: Ja!

Announcer: Join us again next time for Gut Getasten With Helga & Inga, Auf Wiedersehn!

Scripture reference for discussion: James 1: 12 "Blessed is the man who preservers under trial, because when he has stood the test, he will receive the crown of life that God has promised to those who love him."

1Peter1: 6-7 "In this you greatly rejoice, though now for a little while you may had to suffer grief in all kinds of trials. These have come so that your faith—of greater worth than gold, which perishes even though refined by the fire—may be proved genuine and may result in praise, glory and honor when Jesus Christ is revealed."

9. GUT GETASTEN WITH HELGA AND INGA WEISBERG Episode two (a skit on complaining)

"Gut Getasten" is pronounced: goot ge-taste-in.

Players:	Four; Helga, Inga, announcer, and guest
Props:	Helga and Inga's costumes—make them German looking

A table with the following items on it: kitchen tools, bowls, seasonings, table, one cookie, two steins with hot cocoa

One stretchable net—which is already attached to them both (a child's toy hammock works great)

One toy baby

Character analysis: Helga and Inga are two very jolly sisters from Germany who host their own cooking show. They do more talking than cooking and in the end, help to solve the problems of the studio guest. They are very close, rarely argue with each other and can tell tall tales about their homeland. Have fun with these two, the sillier the better and a German accent is imperative.

*Beer stein dance routine: The beer stein dance routine is were Helga and Inga bump their steins together, take a drink, bump their bottoms together then shout "Ja!" simultaneously.

Opening scene: Helga and Inga are at the table stage center mixing the pretend contents of their bowls.

GUT GETASTEN WITH HELGA AND INGA Episode two

Announcer: And now, it's time for everybody's favorite foreign culinary duo, Helga and Inga Weissberg.

(Spot on Helga and Inga at the table)

Helga: Guten tag! Welkommen again to Gut Getasten, I am Helga.

Inga: Unt I am Inga! Unt we have a voonderbar show for you tonight, keeping in mind the usual flair.

Helga: Ja, which is helping our studio guests with their problems through the words of our good Lord.

Inga: So, let's scoot to it and invite our studio guest, _____.

(Spot on guest with baby)

Helga & Inga: Welkommen! So good to have you on the show, unt what a darling kinder, ein lamb! Liebschen!

Guest: Thank you, it's great to be here.

Helga: Good. Now tell us, how is life in the world of a new mommy?

Guest: Oh fine, just fine.

Helga & Inga: Really?

Guest: Yes really, everything is just wonderful.

(Helga and Inga speak in German rapidly. Then do the special*beer stein dance.)

Helga & Inga: Ja!

Inga: It's okay, you can tell us the truth.

Helga: Ja, we don't believe you!

Inga: It's that your arms are tired from holding your kinder day in and day out isn't it?

Guest: No really, it's not that.

Helga: Inga! Let's spell our mommy friend and put the little Liebschen in our schluden!

Inga: Gut!

(Helga and Inga take baby and put it in a sling strung between them—it already has a toy cat in it.)

Helga: See, plenty of room right there next to Boots. Unt he'll keep the kinder warm too.

Inga: Okay now let's talk straight. Why so glum?

Helga: Ja, what gives frau?

Guest: Well, I just went to my class reunion and everyone there had new babies, just like me but they also had every carrier, stroller, back pack and bottle warmer known to man, and I felt terrible that I didn't have any of that stuff for my baby, and I couldn't afford to go get it all for him either. I felt like a bad mom and I was embarrassed.

Helga: Oh boy! The Good Book has lots to say about jealousy.

Inga: Not only the Good Book mein schewester, but the book of your very own life.

Helga: Uh ja, Inga, schelst du dem munde, ach tung! Schnell! Schell!

Inga: Nein Helga, I think this could really help our mommy friend.

Helga: Fine, whatever, out with it.

Inga: Okay, it was October fest in our hometown, and Helga wanted so bad to win the all night polka contest.

Helga: Ja, well tell her the prize.

Inga: The prize was lifetime membership to the Schnitzel Pastry Haus and two years worth of Bratwurst. So you can understand why it was so important to her. Anyway, it was known to everyone that Chi Chi and Danny from Frankfurt were going to be there strutting their stuff and be the ones to beat, for they were the best polka dancers in Germany.

Helga: Ja and to top it all off, Danny had once been my schatzi-poo from the year before.

Inga: So, Helga was insane with jealousy, and was in need of a good polka partner and the only one she could find who was brave enough to challenge Chi Chi and Danny was a gypsy goat juggler named Horst.

Guest: What happened?

Inga: The dancing went on and on until the only two polka dancing couples remaining were Chi Chi and Danny and Helga and Horst and it became obvious that neither couple would give up. So Helga got greedy and did something rash…

Helga: In my defense, the goat juggler was getting clumsy from fatigue and I needed to perk the gepoopstick up. Besides, someone had to do something to impress the judges.

Inga: Right, so she grabbed him by the ankles and began to spin him over her head like a cowgirl's lasso.

Guest: Did it work? Did they win the contest?

Helga: Well yes, and no.

Inga: Everyone stopped what he or she was doing including Chi Chi and Danny so yes, they won.

Helga: my creativity and the beauty in my interpretive polka dancing astonished them all.

Inga: Ja, but the force of the spinning was so great that it lifted both Helga and Horst off their feet like a helicopter and they flew right into the judge's table.

Guest: But you won all the Schnitzel and Bratwurst you could ever want forever.

Helga: No, the goat juggler ran off with all the Bratwurst and the Schnitzel Haus membership card leaving me behind to gather my pride with two broken arms.

Inga: Right, so heed God's warning in Proverbs 15: 25 "A greedy man brings trouble to his family, but he who hates bribes will live."

Holga: Ja, so learn from my lessons, young mommy, and be glad you've got two arms to hold your baby. It could be worse.

Inga: But I know something that might help you feel better.

Helga & Inga: A liebkuchen! (*Inga hands the guest a cookie and then Helga and Inga do the*beer stein dance*)

Helga: That's all for tonight's show. See you next time.

Inga: Auf weidersehn!

Scripture reference for discussion: Philippians 2: 14-16 "Do everything without complaining or arguing so that you may become blameless and pure, children of God without fault in a crooked and depraved generation, in which you shine like stars in the universe as you hold out the word of life—in order that I may boast on the day of Christ that I did not run or labor for nothing."

Romans 15: 13 "May the God of hope fill you with all joy and peace as you trust in him, so that you may over flow with hope by the power of the Holy Spirit."

10. CLIVE THE HOPEFUL PIRATE Episode one: a skit on never giving up hope

Players:	Three; Capt. Clive, Shipstead, and one person to work props
Props:	Inflatable raft or makeshift raft
	Jolly roger flag with SOS on it
	Two pirate costumes—the more tattered the better
	A shark made out of cardboard
	A fishing pole
	A sea gull made out of construction paper with a long pole & fishing line to make the bird fly
	A life ring with "Hope" written on it
	Squirt guns filled with water for audience to spray on Shipstead and Captain Clive when Shipstead exclaims, "look a storm is coming in." Prepare the audience of this necessary participation before skit begins.

Character analysis: Clive is a pirate captain with a cheerful disposition. He never lets anything get him down and is oblivious to trouble. Shipstead is a pessimist and angry at the world.

Opening scene: Two pirates on makeshift raft in the ocean.

CLIVE THE HOPEFUL PIRATE

Captain: (*drawing a deep breath*) Ah, Shipstead, just smell that salt air.

Shipstead: Arg! Captain Clive, we've been drifting about on this raft for weeks with no land insight, no food or fresh water. The sun mercilessly blistering our tender flesh, and you have the gall to breathe deep of the stench in the air and enjoy it! Arg! Arg!

Captain: Ah, Shipstead, always the pessimist. Can't you see the excitement in our predicament? This is an opportunity to test what we are made of, to see if we are really pirates or merely cowardly mice hiding in the grain barrel.

Shipstead: Of all the shipmates in the whole world, I had to survive the storm with *you*, Captain Hopeful, Captain everything-will-be-alright. Look at me, me gots the scurvy, and me legs bow out from the rickets. Me skins peeling off! The sea buzzards are circling our raft waiting to greedily consume my flesh! Arg! Arg!

A bird on string is swung above them, Shipstead swats at it)

Captain: Indeed, that reminds me; I'm feeling a tad hungry. Why don't you be a friend and cast out a line to catch us some fish.

Shipstead: With what shall we cook it?

Captain: Cook it? Were you raised in a barn, Shipstead? We shall fillet it and eat it raw. Sushi, you see, is a fine delicacy.

Shipstead: Capt., have you no nerves left in yer own flesh? Can't you see how yer face and lips are swollen to the point of splitting in two?

Captain: Tis but a flesh wound, Shipstead. Now carry on with your angling.

(Shipstead casts out his line)

Shipstead: I got something!

Captain: Yes, very good, pull it in!

(Shipstead reels in a shark)

(Shipstead: Capt.! Shark! Shark! (*Shipstead bravely fights the shark, eventually releasing it back into the sea)*

Captain: That's fine. Pull him in. Perhaps we can share our catch with him.

Shipstead: Capt., have you no grip on reality? Can't you see our desperate situation here? Me thinks yer dedication to yer invisible God in the sky has clouded yer judgment; either that, or yer God is out to kill us!

Captain: Nonsense, He's just not like that. We must maintain our faith, and hope, and never give up.

(Boat rocks, water splashes, and both men struggle to stay on board)

Shipstead: Well, what else could go wrong anyway? Arg! I spoke to soon! A storm is coming in!

(This is the signal for the audience to squirt their water guns at the actors)

Captain: Tis nothing but a squall, we will sail right through.

Shipstead: I don't believe you, WOAH! WOAH!

Captain: Hang on, Shipstead. Don't give up!

(Life ring—S.S. Hope—thrown in)

Captain: Look! There's hope!

Shipstead: It's not worth it anymore! I can't stand to live one more minute! A A A A A A A A!

(Shipstead jumps into the ocean)

Captain: Shipstead! No! No!

(Storm quiets down)

Captain: Very good then. Thanks Lord. What took you so long?

Scripture reference: 1 Corinthians 10: 13 "No temptation has seized you except what is common to man. And God is faithful; he will not let you be tempted beyond what you can bear. But when you are tempted, he will also provide a way out so that you can stand up under it."

Hebrews 10: 23-24 "Let us hold unswervingly to the hope we profess, for he who promised is faithful. And let us consider how we may spur one another on toward love and good deeds."

11. CLIVE THE HOPEFUL PIRATE Episode two: a skit on keeping your faith

Players:	Five; Capt. Clive, Shipstead, two or three natives
Props:	Two pirate costumes—the more tattered the better
	Two to three native costumes
	Two poles stood upright with firewood at the base
	Squirt guns filled with water for audience to spray on Shipstead and Captain Clive when Clive exclaims "look a storm is coming in" Prepare the audience of this necessary participation before skit begins.

Character analysis: Clive, is a cheerful pirate captain, never lets anything get him down, oblivious to trouble. First mate, Shipstead, is a pessimist and angry at the world

Opening scene: Clive staggers on stage holding his life ring.

CLIVE THE HOPEFUL PIRATE

Captain: Ahh, dry land at last. Since the storm, I've been floating along in my survival tube for weeks and it's been lonely. Alas, poor Shipstead, my loyal first mate, gave up and threw himself into the raging waves never to be seen again. I pray, dear Lord, that you would have mercy on that poor soul, as angry and pessimistic as he was and give him a second chance. But to survive the waves, the tempest of a storm, it churned certain death for one without a life ring like mine. But here's to hope and your mercy O' God. Thank you for delivering me to this island.

(Natives approach him at the shore)

Captain: Locals! Hello there friends. Could you be so kind as to direct me to the nearest village where I could do some pillaging and plundering of the good people there and get myself back on my feet?

Natives: Unga bunga.

(The natives roughly take Clive to their camp)

Captain: Yes. Good. They must have understood! God speed men!

(The natives tie Clive up to a stake next to Shipstead)

Captain: Why Shipstead! You're alive! I'm so happy to see you. It's a miracle! How did you ever survive? What an unexpected treat!

Shipstead: Arg! Captain, indeed I survived but for what? To be made into dinner for these cannibals? I'm not sure what's worse, death by shark infested waters or burning at the stake.

Captain: Those are good questions Shipstead, but these fine gentlemen aren't out to get us. I believe they only wish to keep us still while they question us about the civilized world.

Shipstead: What? The salt water has pickled yer brain Captain! Arg! They's not going to question us. They's going to eat us! And not a moment too soon if you ask me. I don't want to suffer one minute longer on this earth. If your God in heaven actually exists, He delights in torturing me, He does! Arg! Arg!

Captain: Curb thy tongue, Shipstead, my God is gracious and merciful to the end. Just look at your good fortune, surviving this far. I'm sure we'll be released in no time.

Shipstead: Why? *(Looking up to the sky)* Why must I spend my last few minutes on earth being tortured by this man? *(Spoken to Clive)* The fire below us will soon be melting your flesh and a shish-ka-bob we will be on the plates of these savages!

Captain: Nonsense! The fire will simply dry out clothes. And shish-ka-bobs sound delicious. I'm nearly starved to death!

Shipstead: Arg! Why do I even try? Ahh! Hurry up you cruel hooligans, more fire, more fire!

Captain: Shipstead, look, there's a storm coming in!

(This is the signal for the audience to squirt their water guns at the actors)

Shipstead: I don't care! I want to die! I want to die! *(Crying)*

Captain: It's raining! Look at the lightning! It's a torrential down pour! Alleluia! We're saved again! The natives are running for cover. They're scared of the lightning! And the fire has burned through the ropes! We're free again!

Shipstead: It can't be true!

Capt. Clive: It is! And your lack of belief will someday be the ruination of you. May I suggest you change your attitude?

Shipstead: Yeah, yeah, maybe you're right, Captain.

Scripture reference: Matthew 21: 21-22 "Jesus replied, 'I tell you the truth, if you have faith and do not doubt, not only can you do what is done to the fig tree, but also you can say to this mountain, 'Go throw yourself into the sea,' and it will be done. If you believe, you will receive whatever you ask for in prayer.'"

12. THE FISHERS OF MEN—FISH'N SHOW (a skit on ministering to others)

Players:	Seven; Bud, Carl, Earl, Mary, and persons 1, 2 & 3
Props:	Inflatable raft
	Two fishing poles
	Tackle
	Cooler
	Outfits for Bud and Carl (fishing vests, hats)
	A single chair off to the side

Character analysis: Bud and Carl are two very simple men who love God and love to fish. They are as laid back as the day is long and seem to be anxious for nothing.

Opening scene: Bud and Carl sitting in their raft, fishing.

THE FISHERS OF MEN FISH'N SHOW

Announcer: It's time for the Fishers of Men Fish'n Show starring Bud Leuellen and Carl Price. Brought to you by Pork-O Bait, the only bait that's guaranteed to create a grease slick on the surface of the water so you can always know where yer bait is even when yer line has drifted.

Bud: Welcome to the Fishers of Men Fish'n Show, I'm Bud Leuellen…

Carl: And I'm Carl Price. How do.

Bud: Me n' Carl are fish'n for the massive King Salmon of the Queen Charlotte Islands of beautiful British Columbia.

Carl: That's right Bud, and hopefully, if we're lucky, we'll snag a wayward human or two. We'll just have to see what turns up though…

(Bud gets a bite on his line)

Bud: Oh boy, fish on Carl! Check it out! He's a fighter!

Carl: You got enough poundage on yer line there Bud? Easy does it, now don't let him break the line…

(Rather than a fish, Bud pulls in "Earl")

Bud: Oh, well I'll be darned Carl. It's a wayward human! What's yer name son?

Earl: I'm Earl, and what's the big idea putting out bait like that? I couldn't resist!

Carl: Well, that's the whole idea Earl. It's Eternal Life Pork-O Bait and it works every time. We're fix'n to help you get right with the Lord. That is, if yer will-ing?

Earl: Well, what does it require?

Bud: Have a seat on the cooler my friend and we'll fill you in.

(Black out—spot on chair, person # 1 monologue)

Person #1: I was running with a rough group of pike in Minnesota's Crane Lake, when Bud and Carl pulled me in. I was angry, not willing to listen. So, they threw me back. I returned to my group but I couldn't stop thinking about what Bud and Carl had said, freedom from my own oppressive guilt. I realized it was the reason I was swimming away. Then, I began to look for their "Eternal Life Pork-O Bait" everywhere I went, hoping they might pull me in again.

(Spot light on Bud and Carl)

Bud: Welcome back. We've decided to change our tackle for a while. Earl here has decided to join us and learn more about Jesus.

Carl: True be that, Bud. And we're glad he did too 'cause he's given us some good pointers on Sockeye salmon and...woah! Fish on! *(Carl struggles to pull in his line)*

Bud: Dad gum Carl! Look at her jump!

Carl: Easy now. She's a dandy!

(Carl pulls in "Mary")

Mary: Hey, what do you think you're doing anyway? What's going on here?

Bud: Looks like we've caught ourselves a feisty one!

Mary: My name is Mary and I know who you guys are! I however, don't want to have anything to do with your wacky religion. I just want to party and have fun while I'm young...

Bud: Cut the line Carl.

(Black out—spot on chair, person #2 monologue)

Person #2: Rainbow trout. They were my downfall. It was always party this, party that. Everything to them was always honky dory! And for a long while, I loved the lifestyle. The carelessness, the selfishness, it was all about me, and I liked it that way. Then one day, and all of a sudden, it wasn't enough anymore. I ate root slime and wiggled in the shallow streambeds like everyone else, but I was kidding myself. I wasn't happy.

(Black out—person #2 is quickly replaced with person #3, spot back on chair)

Person #3: Bud and Carl reeled me in during my darkest hours. For weeks it had been spawn, spawn, spawn. Kokanee really get lost in their work, and like the rest of my school, I had made work my idol. And it was killing me slowly. Sure, I was securing the future of the species, but I felt empty inside. As I looked around at my friends, I saw they were dying too. Jesus gave me hope for a better life on earth and even better, eternal life after that in heaven.

(Spot on Bud and Carl in boat)

Bud: Well, that's all for today's show. We're hoping' you enjoyed The Fishers of Men Fish'n Show as much as we did, we'll see you out on the water, bye.

Carl: Bye now.

Earl: So long.

Scripture reference: Matthew 4: 18-20 "As Jesus was walking along the Sea of Galilee, he saw two brothers, Simon called Peter and his brother Andrew. They were casting a net into the lake, for they were fishermen. 'Come, follow me,' Jesus said, 'and I will make you fishers of men.' At once they left their nets and followed him."

13. SHEEP IN SPACE (a skit on finding Jesus through your shepherd)

Players:	Five; Capt. Ramchop, Nurse Ewe, Professor Intoxicated, the angel and the announcer
Props:	Three costumes for sheep i.e.: white hats with ears and a blackened nose
	A costume for the angel
	A book of life
	A sword
	A fake cigarette and whisky bottle for Professor Intoxicated;
	A nurse's hat for Nurse Ewe

Character analysis: Capt. Ramchop—the captain spends his life in denial. He believes that his crew is nothing short of perfect. *Professor Intoxicated*—a derelict, smart aleck, who's always intoxicated. *Nurse Ewe*—the smartest one of the bunch.

Opening scene: Three chairs facing the audience in a spaceship configuration. Capt. in front—Nurse on left—Prof. on right.

SHEEP IN SPACE

Announcer: It's time for…Sheeeeeep in Spaaaaace! When we last left our crew they were careening through deep space, in search of a place called…heaven.

Captain: Nurse Ewe,

Nurse Ewe: Yes, Capt.

Captain: How goes the navigational report?

Nurse Ewe: Well that depends Capt., if we are moving in the direction of a well-marked space port, then we are way off course, but if this "heaven" really exists somewhere out here, then I'd say we are headed directly toward it.

Captain: Very good, Nurse Ewe. Professor Intoxicated?

Professor: Yes sir!

Captain: Can you give me the status report on any dangerous gasses in and about the area?

Professor: Um yeah, (*blows out smoke from a cigarette*) here's some now.

Captain: Spot on, Professor Intoxicated.

Nurse Ewe: Look Captain! Up ahead there—I think that's it!

Captain: Good show, Nurse Ewe! My goodness, heaven certainly is bright. Adorn protective eyewear crew.

(Sheep put on sunglasses)

Captain: Make sure you're buckled in; we're going in for a landing.

Nurse Ewe: You know I've heard that in heaven there isn't any death, illness, crying…only happiness.

Professor: Party! Party!

(Sheep lean into landing)

Captain: Professor Intoxicated.

Professor: Sir!

Captain: Make a note as to where we parked, H-3.

Professor: Right! P-27.

Captain: Now, I expect a warm welcome. From what I understand this place is big on lambs. Nevertheless, I expect good behavior from us at all times. (*Capt. looks about and sees angel off to the side*) Ah yes…a local, let's ask for directions to the downtown for a bite to eat.

(Sheep approach Angel)

Captain: Pardon me. My crew and I wish to tour this fine establishment.

(Angel lifts sword defensively)

Captain: Wh…with your permission, of course.

Angel: Allow me to check the Lambs Book of Life…

Nurse Ewe: All right! This is going to be a cinch!

Captain: (*spoken to angel*) My good lady, you had me worried there for a moment. (*Spoken to the crew*) Crew, look your best.

Angel: Your names are not in the book. You will not be allowed passage into heaven.

Captain: Surely there must be some mistake. After all, I speak for everyone when I say that we were all lambs at one time.

Professor & Nurse Ewe: Yeah!

Angel: Without faith in the Lord Jesus Christ, who died for all the sins of the world, and a dedication of your heart and life to Him, you are not saved and therefore shall not be permitted into heaven.

Captain: How do we go about inquiring about this…Jesus?

Angel: Through your shepherd.

Captain: Very well then, thank you all the same, we leave in peace.

(*The sheep return to their ship*)

Nurse Ewe: This stinks, Captain Ramchop!

Captain: No, I believe that was the Professor.

Professor: Sorry.

Nurse Ewe: Boy, that place was weird!

Professor: You're telling me, who would have thought that heaven would have so much red tape? Go through my shepherd—sheeesh! That's almost as bad as trying to get the city to issue you a building permit.

Captain: Indeed, it has left me in a quandary. Perhaps heaven is a bigger, more complicated place than we previously imagined. Let's investigate this further…

Announcer: And so, concludes another adventure of Sheeeeeep in Spaaaaaace.

Scripture reference: John 10: 14-16 "I am the good shepherd; I know my sheep and my sheep know me—just as the Father knows me and I know the Father—and I lay down my life for the sheep. I have other sheep that are not of this sheep pen. I must bring them also. They too will listen to my voice, and there will be one flock and one shepherd."

14. J V C: JESUS VALUE CHANNEL (a skit featuring the Armor of God)

Players: Four; Charmain, Wayne, Mary Beth, and Elizabeth

Props:	A child's Armor of God costume or make your own out of paper or cardboard (sword, helmet, belt, breastplate & shield)
	Charmain's costume—Texan (big and gaudy to the hilt)
	A loaf of French bread
	A carrot
	A bracelet

Character analysis: Charmain is a sugar-sweet Texas debutante, who's got a hearty southern slang and she moves gracefully when displaying the items she has for sale. Her false sugary temperament changes as she's taken to the brink of her tolerance and becomes hostile—revealing her true personality.

Opening scene: Wayne (the producer) is counting down to Charmain for her "on the air" entrance. She is seated stage center with her props near her.

JVC: JESUS VALUE CHANNEL

Wayne: Okay, Charmain, we're on in 5-4-3-2 (*silently*) 1.

Charmain: Hello and welcome back, I'm Charmain Johanningmeyer here today on J V C with today's special value. Typically on J V C we feature products that help you with your heavenly walk. Last week, our featured product (*Charmain displays the bracelet*) was the *"Jesus I Love You"* bracelet in gold and silver. Here let's get a close up Wayne, there are only 200 of these left and you don't want to not have one. It's that important. (*Uses ruler*) It's about a quarter inch in width and is diamond cut. So it catches the light beautifully. A perfect reminder of how sparkly heaven is and at the same time labels you as a lover of Jesus. It's numbers are J-78123 for $59.97 plus shipping and handling and as always J V C takes every major credit card. Oh, what's that Wayne—we're sold out! Now on to today's special value, we have a treat for you, an ensemble of the *"Armor of God"*. Now just look at this. It has everything you could ever need from now on to ensure your place next to the heavenly throne, because this armor will protect you from the spiritual evil one. Here we have the Belt of Truth. (*Displays the belt*) always tell the truth now. And here is the Breastplate of Righteousness (*displays the breastplate*) and just look at the craftsmanship. This literally took months—

Wayne: Hours! (*Shouted from back stage*)

Charmain: —Hours to construct. The Shield of Faith. *(Displays shield)* This will help keep you strong during those troubled times which we all endure, honey. Also, protecting you from your deepest fears, doubt, and discouragement. And the Helmet of Salvation *(displays the helmet)* it will help keep your thoughts pure, no naughty thoughts now. And who could go into battle without the Sword of the Spirit? (Displays sword) And what's so nice about our J V C designed Sword of the Spirit, is how it is a multifaceted tool which can be used in your kitchen when you're not fighting off temptation and spiritual assaults. Watch how it slices French bread *(demonstrate)* and it also juliennes carrots *(demonstrate)*. This is definitely a "must have" for your home. No good Christian homemaker should be without the *"Armor of God"* ensemble. The Sword alone makes the money you will spend worth it. Now I understand that we have a call on the line, this is Mary Beth from Sarasota, welcome Mary Beth.

Mary Beth: Hello Charmain.

Chairman: Hello, welcome to J V C. Did you buy something today?

Mary Beth: Yes I did, but I just wanted to say that you're just the prettiest Texan woman I've ever seen and I always watch J V C when you are hosting because it's like you're just my bestest friend!

Charmain: Why thank you, Mary Beth, aren't you just the sweetest thing. Now tell the viewers what it is you bought that's going to strengthen your walk to the Golden Gates of Heaven.

Mary Beth: Oh yes! I bought the *"Jesus I Love You"* bracelet for my mother; sister and twin daughters and I feel so secure and happy in knowing that the women of my family are going to heaven. And I know you're going to be there too Chairman!

Charmain: Thank you. Now isn't that nice? Now for all of you who are watching and are curious about what J V C is all about and why you should buy our products. Just stay tuned for a while and we just know that you'll want to be a part of our crusade. Okay, another caller. Hello, you're on J V C's special value hour. Who is this?

Elizabeth: I'm Elizabeth.

Charmain: Welcome Elizabeth. Where are you from?

Elizabeth: Portland, Maine.

Charmain: And what items did you purchase today from J V C?

Elizabeth: Well, none. And I think you're way off in stating that any of these products are going to help anyone to get into heaven. The jewelry, the "*Armor of God*" costume, those things are objects that have no value after you die and they don't guarantee any kind of passage into heaven.

Charmain: Well, aren't we pious and righteous? If you think you know everything my little Pharisee, then I wish you luck in the afterlife—you're going to need it.

Elizabeth: I don't think so, but you need help and so do all of your viewers if you think that anything that is not of your heart, your mind and soul, the free things, will get you grace from God.

Charmain: Wayne, I think we've heard enough from little "Miss Bertha Better-Than-You. Look at me, I'm in the first pew!" (*Makes a" cut across throat" motion to Wayne.*)

Elizabeth: See what I mean? That isn't Christian-like at all—the way you're talking to me…

(*Charmain grabs sword and waves it, pounds it on the table*)

Charmain: Wayne! You good for nothing producer! How could you let a caller like that get through? I said cut her off!

(*Charmain stops suddenly, realizing her mistake, looks at cameras and collects herself, shakily puts down sword*)

Charmain: Well, it appears we're out of time. I doubt I'll be seeing you at 11: 00 for the "Fruits of the Spirit" elegant dinner and flatware promotional because, I'm sure, that as of a few minutes ago, I'm out of a job. So, bye bye.

Scripture reference: The armor of God can be found in Ephesians Chapter Six, verses Ten through Eighteen.

1 Corinthians 13: 1-3 "If I speak in the tongues of men and of angels, but have not love, I am only a resounding gong or a clanging cymbal. If I have the gift of prophecy and can fathom all mysteries and all knowledge, and if I have faith that can move mountains, but have not love, I am nothing. If I give all I possess to the poor and surrender my body to the flames, but have not love I gain nothing."

15. THE TWO HEADED POLITICIAN (a skit on taking a stand)

Players: Five; Howard, Kenneth and reporters 1,2 &3

Props: Costume for Howard and Kenneth—a very large pair of pants, shirt, and tie. Both of the players need to fit into the outfit and appear as though they are a human with one body and two heads.

Character analysis: Kenneth is a liberal Democrat, while his counterpart, Howard, is a conservative Republican. Because they have each other to balance their views, they have no fear of saying exactly what's on their minds. They are power hungry and self seeking, looking to please everyone. The reporters can be dressed in anything and are seated out within the audience, standing when they speak.

Opening scene: Howard and Kenneth enter and stop center stage to answer questions at a press conference.

THE TWO-HEADED POLITICIAN

Kenneth & Howard: Thank you for your warm welcome. Remember "two heads are better than one"—we're your man for State Senate!

Kenneth: I'll take a question from the man in the yellow shirt there…

Reporter #1: Kenneth, what is your stand on the water level problem throughout our reservoirs, and if elected, what would you do to solve this?

Kenneth: Well, obviously, lack of water means a great number of native fish will die, I would require all citizens to be taxed an additional 10% on property taxes with a 10% discount for those who could prove that they've taken fewer than a dozen or so showers in the past year. Conservation is the key.

Reporter #2: What about you Howard, how would you handle the crisis?

Howard: When I think of a lack of water, I think of fewer family trips to the reservoir to water ski and bond as a family unit. Kenny here may say he doesn't care about water skiing but he's laughing his head off every time I'm out there and he's also enjoying the ride to boot. Recreation is important and I'd give anyone who could catch double their legal limit of crappie and bass, a break on their taxes. There's just too many fish out there. Decrease the number of fish inhabiting the water, and you've increased the livability of the fish that survive.

Reporter #2: What about the lawn mower issue. Should the gas-powered lawn mower be made illegal and only electric lawn mowers be allowed?

Howard: Okay, have you ever tried to cut grass with an electric mower? You may as well flip a piece of pasta over your grass and get just as far. They don't work for didily. And besides, the roar of the mowers engine on bright Saturday mornings is therapeutic to the overworked American man. He needs this kind of outlet and exercise.

Kenneth: Right. Those of you who know Howie, know just how much he cares about exercise. Nada! Of course, I support the electric lawn mower. It decreases pollution and as far as it's efficiency, I believe all grasses should be allowed to grow wildly and naturally without any cutting. The taller the better. Weed power!

Reporter #1: What about wood stoves? Campaign finance reform? Tax exemptions? Non-smoking rules on international flights?

Howard: No?

(Gasp from all reporters)

Howard: Um…

Kenneth: He means that I mean no, or yes, or actually, no.

Reporter #2: The mosquito problem? Negative campaigning? Dogs and cats living together?

Howard: Yes, no.

Kenneth: Yes, yes, no.

Reporter #1: Terrorism? Global warming? SARS? West Nile virus?

Howard & Kenneth: Yes, no, yes, no, no.

Reporter #2: Shoes that don't fit, studded snow tires after April 1st, small pox vaccine, enriched flour, over crowded prisons, third world famine?

Howard & Kenneth: Yes, no, yes, no!

Reporter #3: Howard, if you and Kenneth are elected, how will you be able to make decisions in the senate with such opposite opinions on everything.

Kenneth: We are masters of negotiation.

Howard: That's right bro—you've never seen anything like us and you never will again! We are a medical miracle!

Kenneth: Evolutionary genius!

Howard: Two minds in one body and our only purpose is to serve you.

Kenneth: When you have both sides of the political spectrum to debate all your issues for you, why would you need anyone else?

Howard: We can't guarantee that we'll ever be able to agree on anything.

Kenneth: Or stand together on any issues.

Howard: But at least you know that despite your party affiliation, your voice will be heard. I know I can say whatever I want because Kenneth here will always be there to patronize me.

Kenneth: And likewise, Howard covers all my conservative whims, so I never have to worry about saying the wrong thing in a press conference. I can be as liberal as I want.

Reporter #1: These guys or I mean guy, are great! How could you go wrong voting for them?

Reporter #2: They are so knowledgeable about all the issues. Their two minds together will always keep our state in the middle of all the issues, never having to take a stand.

Reporter #3: That's right! And what's best is we'll only have to pay one salary through our taxes for the two of them. It makes perfect sense! Boy! I wish I were those guys, and never had to stand one way or the other on any issue.

Reporter #1: No kidding. That's a good way to lose friends.

Reporter #2: Three cheers for the Two-Headed Politician! Hip—Hip—Hooray!

Scripture reference: Matthew 5: 34-37 "But I tell you, do not swear at all: either by heaven, for it is God's throne; or by earth for it is his foot stool; or by Jerusalem for it is the city of the great King. And do not swear by your head, for you cannot make even one hair on your head either white or black. Simply let your 'Yes' be 'Yes' and your 'No' be 'No'; anything beyond this comes from the evil one."

16. THE FACADE FAMILY (a skit on appearing perfect)

Players:	Five; Mom, Father, Jonathan, Sarah, and young Jeremy
Props:	Mom's costume—something tidy
	Dad's costume—shirt and tie
	Jonathan—anything teen like
	Sarah—anything racy, sweater to put over it
	Toast and a newspaper on a small table
	Four chairs off to the side, which will serve as the family car.

Character analysis: Mom cares about nothing but looking like she's the perfect mother of a perfect family. Dad is detached, aloof and reclusive. Jonathan is eager to please his mother. Sarah is rebelling against her mother.

Opening scene: Mom is trying to get family ready for church. She's calling to them from the kitchen.

THE FACADE FAMILY

Mom: *(calling off stage)* Jonathan, hurry up, you're going to make us late! *(To herself)* I swear that boy spends more time in the bathroom than all his female relatives combined.

(Father enters)

Mom: Hello dear, coffee?

Dad: Sure. *(Reads paper)*

(Daughters enters)

Mom: You will not be wearing that! You'll make us all look like trashy low life's. Back to your room—now!

Jonathan! Get down here to eat now! I will not have you passing out in Sunday school again and making a scene! *(Spoken to father)* Toast dear?

Dad: *(from behind paper)* Uh, huh.

(RING, RING beckons a telephone)

Mom: Now who could that be at 8: 00 on Sunday morning? Only the most inconsiderate of people would call at such a busy time. *(Spoken very sweetly)* Hello, the Fau-cie-aude Family, lady of the house speaking. Well of course we'll bring Brock home from church. No, no, it will be no problem at all—okay—very good, bye now! That was Marilyn, needing a ride home from church for her son Brock—figures she'd ask for help—she can't do anything on her own—always troubling everyone else. And it will be a miracle alone if we can even find Brock after church. That child can't find his way out of a paper bag.

(Daughter enters)

Mom: That's not much better, Sarah. Well, it's too late now; you'll just have to bring shame to us all. To the car!

(Jonathan follows, finally)

Jonathan: How do I look, Mom?

(All four sit in car)

Mom: Lovely, Jonathan, all your time in the bathroom paid off.

Sarah: Mom, I don't want to go to church, it's all a big fake out. You know everyone there is only being nice for show.

Mom: Now that's not true, Sarah, just look at us. *(Mom turns her attention out the window)* There's Sheridan Moore…with a new beau on her arm…I swear, she has more boyfriends than shoes in her closet, *(sweetly)* hello! *(Waves)*

(Car is parked, all players exit car)

Mom: *(to father)* Straighten your tie dear, you don't want to look disheveled.

Young Jeremy: Hello, Mrs. Facade.

Mom: That's Fau-cie-aude, young Jeremy! *(Mom rolls her eyes dramatically)* Now smiles everyone, smiles!

Scripture reference: Matthew 6: 1 "Be careful not to do your 'acts of righteous' before men, to be seen by them. If you do, you will have no reward from your Father in heaven."

17. G D H I A—GLOBAL DISGRUNTLED HOLIDAY ICON ASSOCIATION (a skit on the true meanings behind our celebrated holidays)

Players:	Six; Uncle Sam, Easter Bunny, Leprechaun, Cupid, Santa, and the Tooth Fairy
Props:	Pulpit and a gavel
Character analysis:	Uncle Sam: governmental
	Easter Bunny: feels unappreciated
	Leprechaun: feels invisible
	Cupid: angry, tough
	Santa: soft-hearted, pushover
	Tooth Fairy: an encourager, soft spoken

Opening scene: Uncle Sam pounds his gavel to gain the attention of his audience. The other characters are seated within the audience and stand when it is their turn to speak.

GLOBAL DISGRUNTLED HOLIDAY ICONS ASSOCIATION—G D H I A

Uncle Sam: This meeting of the G D H I A will now come to order. Order please, order I say. The issue has been raised that the typical holiday calendar year of characters are being overthrown by the true meanings behind their season and therefore, striking the identity of the associated pagan icons. The floor will now recognize discussion. Yes, Easter Bunny.

Easter Bunny: Yeah—this just stinks! Everybody knows Easter is the day Jesus Christ overcame death and rose again after being crucified on the cross but it seems that nobody knows that the Easter Bunny is a pagan traditional symbol of fertility, which originated out of Germany. People encourage their children to eat my chocolates and hide my colorful eggs but at the same time send their children to church where they worship Jesus. It makes me feel, well, used.

Leprechaun: Aye! And what about me? My whole existence depends on folklore and me pot-o-gold! If too many more people realize that St. Patty's day is a celebration of the work of Saint Patrick the martyred missionary. I'm sure to disappear!

(Arguing and agreement among all patrons)

Uncle Sam: *(pounding gavel)* Order, order, I say!

Santa: Now wait a minute everyone. Sure, I admit it's a lot of giggles to be idolized during our special times of year, but what's so wrong with people knowing the truth about us?

Cupid (with cigar): Oh sit down, you goody-two-boots. Why don't you go take your belly full of jelly and go clean up the mess that your reindeer made out in the grass.

Santa: I'm going to remember this Cupid, your #1 on my naughty list.

Cupid: Oooo, I'm so scared!

Uncle Sam: Enough! Now let's handle this unemotionally. Cupid, one more outburst like that and I'll have to have Frankenstein and Wolf Man remove you from these premises.

Tooth Fairy: Permission to speak, sir.

Uncle Sam: Yes, Tooth Fairy.

Tooth Fairy: All we can do is continue to work hard and strive to muffle the depth of these Christian holidays with fantasy and materialism. Together I just know we can make a difference!

(Applause from all characters)

Uncle Sam: Well done, Tooth Fairy! Indeed, let us not give up. Persevere, my icon peers. Let's hit the streets and get back to work!

(Cupid raises fist to Santa, who gets scared and runs. Cupid chuckles and chews cigar)

Scripture reference: John 8: 31-3 "To the Jews who had believed him, Jesus said, 'If you hold to my teaching, you are really my disciples. Then you will know the truth, and the truth will set you free.'"

18. JINGLE SKIT

The Jingle Skit is done around Christmas time and involves any three characters you wish from the following list. The actors will portray their character in mannerism and costume and sing common Christmas carols. What's so funny about the skit is that the characters listed are either well known for their inability to speak clearly i.e.: Frankenstein, caveman. Therefore they only grunt or mumble out the songs or they are known for some specific characteristic i.e.: Goliath-fierce warrior, and therefore spend their stage time acting out their character. If it's Goliath, he should wave his sword at the audience and demand that they sing along. If another character is holding a candle, that character could interact with Frankenstein *(who is afraid of fire)* and cause a scene in that way. In any case this skit is simple to create and even simpler to improvise, just have fun.

Possible characters:

*Goofy	*Caveman
*The Hulk	*Donald Duck
*A baby	*A foreigner who can't speak English
*Frankenstein	*A Viking
*Goliath	*Marilyn Monroe

19. MICHAL'S SCHOOL OF INTERPRETIVE DANCE (a skit on being yourself and praising God your own way)

Players: Five; Michal, King David, and three other dancers

Props: Michal's costume—make it hippie like

                      King David's costume—make him royal

                      Dancer's costumes—exercise clothes

Character analysis: Michal believes that her interpretive dance moves are how everyone should express himself or herself. Also, she can hardly tolerate her husband King David. Everything he does is a horrific embarrassment to her. King David loves God more than he loves his wife. He's going to do whatever he wants regardless of what she says. After all, he is the King.

Opening scene: Michal is gaining the attention of her class who are warming up with some pre-dance stretching.

MICHAL'S SCHOOL OF INTERPRETIVE DANCE

Michal: Okay, okay people, eyes on me. Welcome to Michal's School of Interpretive Dance. I'm your instructor, Michal, Queen of Israel, but I want you to think of me as your guide into a bigger world of creativity and self-realization. Let's begin with stretches, and up (*Michal reaches gracefully to ceiling. The three dancers follow her every move*) touch the sun, ouch, (*pulls her hands back*) it burned our fingers. And down, (*she bends down*) fingers into the earth. Find a stinkbug—ooh! (*Sniffs her fingers*) It stinks! Flick it away! (*Comes to an upright position*) All right now, what a delicious warm-up that was! Now, as you know, here in Israel, we spend a lot of time praising the God of Abraham, Isaac, Jacob and my husband, David. However, it is my theory that there is a proper way to praise, and it is in organized synchronicity. Now, in the morning we are to thank God for the day and the air we breathe with a wide sweep of the right arm and a lift as we inhale and reach outward as we exhale (*she demonstrates and the class follows*). Yes. Good. Again now, sweep and lift, reach—beautiful. At noon, let us thank God for the bounty of our crops with a stoop to pick the produce and a chop-chop and frying motion as we prepare it (she *demonstrates again and the class follows)* ahh, yes. And finally at night, we dance in a controlled fashion as we soak in the glowing rays of the moon and stars from the heavens with a twirl and a pulling of the beams toward ourselves (*she twirls and pulls an imaginary rope toward herself, the dancers follow but King David is beginning to lose interest and starts to do his own moves)*. Okay, from the top—sweep the air—lift our breath—exhale and reach—pick the crops—chop and prepare—good. Then, twirl and pull. Now up the tempo, 5, 6, 7, 8—sweep and lift—reach and pick—chop and prepare—twirl and pull.

(David is doing his own thing, and beginning to toss off layers of clothes.)

Michal: Um, David honey, what do you think you're doing over there? Those aren't the moves the rest of us are doing!

David: I'm praising God in my own way. I'm dancing according to how I feel. God knows my heart, regardless of my moves.

Michal: Honey, you're embarrassing me, and everyone around you.

David: I don't care. My dance is all about my love for God and I have nothing to hide—God sees inside my heart—He knows if I mean it or not.

(Dancers begin to get confused and stumble over their moves as they watch both Michal and David)

Michal: Pay no attention to my defiant husband over there class. He's determined to make a fool of himself today. So let's take it from the top—5, 6, 7, 8—and sweep and…

(The other dancers give up on Michal's instruction and watch David, encouraging him with applause)

Michal: Excuse me; I'm the instructor here! This is my class! David stop! (*Stomps her feet*) You look like a lunatic. I won't tolerate this kind of unorganized interpretive dance in my studio! (*Michal realizes that no one is listening to her*) HUMPH!! Fine, I'm leaving…here I go…I'm almost gone!

(*She leaves out the door; the class continues to applaud David who takes a dramatic bow*)

Scripture reference: The story of Michal and her relationship with King David is found in the book of Second Samuel, Chapter Six.

20. SAMANTHA SUPER CHRISTIAN #1 (a skit on the definition of agape love)

Players:	One; Samantha
Props:	Samantha's outfit—make it that of a nerdy super hero
	A sign that says "Agape=Unconditional love" on one side and "A guppy=little fish" on the other side.

Character analysis: Samantha Super Christian is a super hero who feels that the church, and for that matter, the whole world, desperately needs her insight and protection. She talks with a distinctive speech impediment. One that's described as a lisp, spoken out the side of her mouth.

Opening scene: Samantha enters boisterously, flapping her cape and shouting "*up, up and away!*" She finally takes her place at center stage.

SAMANTHA SUPER CHRISTIAN #1

Greetings. We've never met. I'm Samantha Super Christian. I am a super hero and I'm taking time out of my busy schedule of saving souls for Christ to bring you the word of the day and the church update. First and foremost—God's blessings on you all—and as you depart this evening—God speed. Our word of the day is "Agape" (*she holds up her sign*) described in our sacred Bible as being unconditional love—love with no end, no pre-requisite, unearned, undeserved, an under-estimated kind of love that God extends to us, His children with no strings attached. God loves you when you're sleeping, He knows when you're awake, He knows when you've been bad or good, so be good for goodness sake. Regardless of whether we're good or not, God always loves us. Satisfied?

All right—"Agape" also has another meaning, one that's often overlooked but still will surprise you when you realize its commonness. (*She flips sign over*) agape is also a tiny little fish that children often keep in tiny aquariums at home or at pre-school. Cute little fellas!

Okay, on to updates with the church and it's parish. Our pastor has upped his usual donation earmarked for missions giving. He says "up yours." Also, several of our ladies groups will be casting off their old clothing for the church fund-raiser. You can see them in action or join in on Tuesdays after 3p.m. Lastly—be sure to attend tonight's services. Miss Bertha Belch, a missionary from Africa, will be speaking tonight. Come and hear Bertha Belch all the way from Africa.

With that, I say sayonara sisters and brothers. Remember, love one another! Up, Up and AWAY! (*Samantha exits*)

Scripture reference: John 13: 1 "It was just before the Passover feast. Jesus knew that the time had come for him to leave this world and go to the Father. Having loved his who were in the world, he now showed them the full extent of his love."

Romans 13: 9-10 "The commandments, 'Do not commit adultery, Do not murder, Do not steal, Do not covet and whatever other commandment there may be, are summed up in this one rule: Love your neighbor as yourself.' Love does no harm to its neighbor. Therefore love is the fulfillment of this law."

21. SAMANTHA SUPER CHRISTIAN #2 (a skit on the definition of "Levite")

Players:	One; Samantha
Props:	Samantha's costume: nerdy super hero
	A sign that says "Levite" on one side and "Levite=tight jeans on teens" on the other. A picture of young teens in tight jeans can be found in any magazine or clothing catalogs and is a cute addition to the sign.

Character analysis: Samantha Super Christian is a super hero who feels that the church, and for that matter, the world desperately needs her insight and protection. She talks with a distinctive speech impediment. One that's described as a lisp, spoken out the side of her mouth.

Opening scene: Samantha enters boisterously, flapping her cape and shouting "up, up and away!" She finally takes her place at center stage.

SAMANTHA SUPER CHRISTIAN #2

Greetings and salutations once again. I am Samantha Super Christian, your local super hero working my strenuous schedule of saving souls for Christ but allowing time to bring you the Gatherings word of the day and our church update.

First things first, God loves you, I love God, so therefore vicariously, I love you too.

Our word of the day is "Levite" *(she holds up her sign)*. The Bible tells us that a Levite was one of the twelve tribes of Israel who were responsible for taking care of the Ark of the Covenant. You know, like keeping it sacred in its maintenance, transportation, storage and so on, get it? Okay now, Levite also has another meaning, *(she flips her sign over)* which is a very tiny pair of jeans. Wearable only by prepubescent teens.

Now, on to updates—

This coming Sunday, our own youth pastor will be singing "I Will Not Pass This Way Again" which will bring obvious pleasure to the congregation.

Ladies, don't forget the rummage sale this weekend. It's a chance to get rid of those things not worth keeping around the house. Don't forget your husbands.

Lastly, the Low Esteem Support Group will meet Thursday in the fellowship hall at 7p.m. Please use the back door.

With that, I say so long Sisters and Brothers. Remember beloved; love one another, 1 John 7 & 8! Up, Up and AWAY! *(Samantha exits)*

Scripture reference: A description of who the Levites were and their appointed duties are explained in the book of Numbers, Chapter One verses Forty-Seven through Fifty-Four.

22. SAMANTHA SUPER CHRISTIAN #3 (a skit on the definition of "Philistine")

Players: One; Samantha

Props: Samantha's costume is that of a nerdy super hero

Two signs, one with a face shot of Goliath on it and the word "Philistine" written above him, the other with the same face shot of Goliath but with glasses and gray hair, pulled up into a bun. The words "Phyllis Steen" should be written above the second picture.

Character analysis: Samantha Super Christian is a super hero who feels that the church, and for that matter, the world desperately needs her insight and protection. She talks with a distinctive speech impediment. One that's described as a lisp spoken out the side of her mouth.

Opening scene: Samantha enters boisterously, flapping her cape and shouting "up, up and away!" She finally takes her place at center stage.

SAMANTHA SUPER CHRISTIAN #3

Sisters and Brothers in Christ, I salute you once again as I, Samantha Super Christian, takes time out of my busy schedule of defeating evil to bring you the word of the day and our church update.

Our word of the day is "Philistine" (*displays sign of Goliath*) By definition—Philistines—were a migrating people who lived in the area of Canaan during Old Testament times who frequently warred with the Israelites.

Goliath was a Philistine. The Philistines also were the naughty people who poked Samson's eyes out in Judges 16: 4-21, get the picture? Now Philistine holds strong personal meaning to me, as it was the name of my third grade teacher, Mrs. Phyllis Steen, in my home-town of Salishan. (*She displays second picture of "Phyllis Steen"*) She has since passed away. She was strict and non-emotional, a real sergeant. When it came to times tables, many of my irreparable childhood scars originated from Mrs. Steen's class and hence has made me what I am today, a protector of good, a supporter of the underdog, a pillar of righteousness for all to admire. At the tender age of eight, I disliked Mrs. Steen and her viperous tactics. Now I raise a cup to her for she made me what I am—to you Mrs. Phyllis Steen, I've heard Hell is warm, I hope it is at least as much for you.

Now, on to our church updates…

Ladies Bible study will be held Thursday morning at 10 a.m. All ladies are invited to lunch in the fellowship hall when the B S is done.

Irving Benson and Jessie Carter were married on January 11th. So ends a friendship that began in their school days.

Our beloved parishioner, Barbara, remains in the hospital and needs more blood donors for more transfusions. She is also having trouble sleeping and requests tapes of the church's board meetings.

Lastly, our Worriers Anonymous Support Group meets Friday nights at 6 p.m. They encourage you not to let worry kill you off, let the church help. With that I bid you so long! Up, Up and AWAY! (*Samantha exits*)

Scripture reference: A good description of Goliath and the Philistines is found in the book on First Samuel, Chapter Seventeen.

23. THE JUSTIFICATION POLICE (a skit on justifying your actions)

Players:	Seven; Jackson Mahoney, Pep Stapleton, jogger, woman at well, gift woman, the mayor and a caveman.
Props:	Costume for Jackson Mahoney—trench coat, Humphrey Bogart hat and handcuffs
	Costume for Pep Stapleton—anything that could be viewed as opposite from Jackson, like a hippy or a slob.
	Costume for jogger—sweat suit and doughnut
	Gift Lady—several bags of gifts, shopping bags
	Wishing Well Lady—bag of coins
	Cave Man—shaggy hair, bare feet, tattered oversized shirt made of fur or the like.

Character analysis: Jackson Mahoney goes by the book, takes his career seriously. Has an intense drive to see justice be done. His partner, Pep, annoys Jackson. Pep Stapleton is a nonconformist, finds joy in annoying his partner. He is interested in seeing justice being served but won't lose a moment of sleep if it isn't.

Opening scene: Jackson is talking directly to the audience while Pep is at the table tossing snack food into his mouth.

THE JUSTIFICATION POLICE

Mahoney: It began as an ordinary day. It ended as extraordinary. My nonconformist partner, Pep Stapleton, and I were just finishing up our paperwork from the prior day when the call came in, my name is Mahoney, Jackson Mahoney, I'm a Justification Policeman.

(RING, RING beckons the phone. Jackson grabs the phone before Stapleton does)

Mahoney: This is Mahoney.

Mayor: Yes, Jackson? This is the Mayor I need your help! Citizens all over our fair city are committing random acts of selfishness and self-indulgence without any clear justification. What's worse though, the motivation behind these acts stem from feelings of rejection, low self worth and loneliness. Can you help them? Without the correct justification for their actions, our city will become nothing but a free-for-all!

Mahoney: Don't worry Mayor. Help is on the way.

(Pep and Jackson grab hats and head for the door)

Mahoney: (*spoken directly to the audience*) It wasn't hard finding where to begin. The city was infected with rampant unjustification. Everywhere you looked the citizens were acting strangely.

Stapleton: Look Mahoney, there's one now!

(A jogger enters with doughnut)

Mahoney: Pardon me good citizen. May I inquire why you are eating a doughnut while you're jogging?

Jogger: Well, I like doughnuts, but they make me gain weight, so, I figure that if I jog while I eat them, it kind of cancels out that I even ate them in the first place.

Stapleton: Sounds good to me.

Mahoney: Indeed, carry on good citizen, sorry to have troubled you.

Stapleton: Look, there is the shopping center parking lot! That gal is loading her car with lots of gifts. Let's check it out!

Mahoney: Roger.

(*Mahoney and Stapleton approach gift lady*)

Stapleton: Hey, Ma'am, I couldn't help but notice how many boxes of gifts that you're loading into your car. It appears you've spent quite a bit of money today. Can ya tell me why?

Gift Lady: It's easy. You see my husband tells me all the time how we never have any money to do the things I want to do. Then he goes and buys a motorcycle for himself. It made me so angry that I took our credit card and spent the same amount of money on gifts for the kids and I that he spent on that motorcycle. That'll teach him to buy something behind my back again.

Mahoney: Perfect justification Ma'am. Please forgive us for the inconvenience. (*Mahoney and Stapleton turn away from gift lady*) I'm confused Stapleton. The good people of our city all seem perfectly justified in their behavior.

Stapleton: Wait, Mahoney, look there. (*Stapleton points in the direction of the woman at the well*)

Mahoney: Let's roll!

Woman at Wishing Well: (*as she is throwing coins*) And for Jessica...

Mahoney: Pardon us Miss, what's with the bag of coins? Isn't wishing once enough?

Woman at Wishing Well: Not if I'm going to be unselfish about my wishes.

Stapleton: What do you mean?

Woman at Wishing Well: Well, I want to have lots and lots of money, so I can have beautiful clothes and cars and houses like some of the people I know in town. But it's wrong to covet their stuff. So, I'm wishing for me to have all their stuff and that they just had more than they've already got. That makes it okay.

Stapleton: Makes perfect sense.

Mahoney: Good day, Miss.

(Mahoney and Jackson leave the woman at the well)

Stapleton: Well, I guess we better go back to the station, there's nothing for us out here to do.

Mahoney: Pep—our ship may have just come in! Look there.

Caveman chewing on bone: Growl, snort.

(Mahoney and Stapleton approach the caveman)

Stapleton: Yo—Cavey-Dude, what are you doing in the 21st century? Why are you chewing that bone there—and more importantly, where did you get a leg bone like that?

Caveman: Growl, growl.

Stapleton: Did you catch that?

Mahoney: Negative, this guy's going downtown!

(Justification Police cuff Caveman—begin their exit)

Mahoney: (spoken directly to the audience) And so marks the end of another exciting day in the lives of the Justification Police. Tune in next time to hear Officer Stapleton say…

Stapleton: This dude needs a bath!

Mahoney: (spoken directly to the audience) Kind of like someone else I know.

Scripture reference: Romans 8: 33-34 "Who will bring any charge against those whom God has chosen? It is God who justifies. Who is he that condemns? Christ Jesus, who died—more than that, who was raised to life—is at the right hand of God and is also interceding for us."

24. AT HOME ON THE RANGE (a skit on being who you say you are)

Players: Three; Buck, Hal and Lance

Props: Three cowboy costumes

Foot bath

Bubble bath

A cell phone

A romance novel

Moisturizer

Character analysis: Hal and Buck are manly and burly men. They have bowed legs, aching backs and a hundred miles left to ride before they get home and they wouldn't have it any other way. Lance likes the idea of being a cowboy but he doesn't want to give up the easier lifestyle or the comforts of home when out on the prairie. The title of "Cowboy" gives him status. He likes the way it makes him look to others but to jump in with both feet and actually *become* a cowboy causes him too much discomfort.

Opening scene: Three cowboys around a fire.

AT HOME ON THE RANGE

Buck: Well boys, another tiresome but rewarding day running doggies. It doesn't get much better than this.

Hal: Yep, I reckon there are hun'erds of easier lines of work in this britches bus-ten' country of ours. But nothin' beats being a cowboy.

Buck: Yes'um, the dust on yer brow, the sun leathering yer skin—and the sound of the coyote coaxing in her prey and the only thing you've got for a blanket is the light of full moon, yes sir.

Lance: That's right my fellow buckaroos, and I can think of only one thing that's better'n all the things you all mentioned.

Buck & Hal: What's that?

Lance: After a tiresome day of ropin' and ridin', I just love to kick back with a good book and pamper my feet in a motorized foot massager. Even brought bubbles.

(Lance puts foot in bath and gets out a book. Hal and Buck look at each other embarrassed)

Buck: Well now, that's a durn near fancy contraption. It's my opinion that the quiet and ruggedness of the prairie gets a man to thinkin' 'bout the deeper things—God, the meaning of life, the pretty girl he left back home, the meaning of what it is to be a man, and nothing but your thoughts for a pillow.

Hal: Not to mention the conditions that we cowboys have to endure. The fierce sun, wind and dust, injury and the need to survive, makes us what we are, "Cowboys."

Lance: You think so? All that sun sure is great for perking up my color but in the evenings it's moisturize, moisturize! I can barely keep up with the wrinkles that are starting to appear around my eyes, even when I use "Alpha Hydroxy."

Buck: Uh…I don't seem to have that problem.

Hal: Me neither! Anyway I guess I most appreciate the loneliness of the prairie, the lowing of the cattle…

(Ring, Ring beckons a cell phone from inside Lances coat)

Lance: Oh, excuse me. *(Taking out phone)* Hello? Hey Brandy—yeah, I'm great, just living the cowboy life with my two new amigos.

(Hal and Buck are discussing something between them)

Lance: Oh, Hal and Buck, they're great guys, a little on the gamey side, but…

(Buck and Hal stand up and take away Lance's phone)

Lance: Hey! Wait! What are you doing? That's my phone!

(Then, Buck and Hal take away his foot massager. Lance looks scared as they grab for more)

Lance: No! Not my moisturizer! Anything but that! Or my Danielle Steele!

Hal: Listen here Lance—if you're going to say you're a cowboy—then you're gonna have to live like one or else you're going to give us cowboys a bad name.

Lance: But all my stuff! How am I going to live without it?

Buck: It'll be hard at first, I know. I can compare it to halter breaking a horse. You'll get used to it and before long, you'll wonder why you ever cared about foot massagers and cell phones and the like.

Hal: And it's for your own good too. What if you had teamed up with a couple of really angry cowboys tonight? You know the kind, with issues to sort out, instead of good guys like us? And you began to put your feet in a footbath with bubbles?

Lance: Well, I'd give everyone a turn if they wanted, provided they didn't have athlete's foot or a toe fungus.

Hal: Lance, them mean men of the range woulda used you for sightin' in their rifles and justify it by thinking they did ya a favor by putting you outta your confused misery.

Lance: Oh, I see, so there's a certain way to live once you've declared yourself a cowboy? Interesting. Not everyone does it you know. I mean walk the walk while they are talkin' the talk. That's kind of like the life a Christian chooses to live. It's a hard life, really hard, but in the end it's supposed to be worth it.

Hal: I declare, Buck, I think he's getting it!

Buck: And on that note—how many people have you seen turn away from our Almighty Father because someone who was supposedly a Christian didn't act like one.

Lance: Yeah, kinda like me. I've only met a couple of Christians in my life and I thought them all to be phony—except maybe you fellas.

(*Hal and Buck look at each other kindly then feel uncomfortable with the sensitivity they are displaying*)

Buck: Well, that's more talkin' than this cowboy usually does in a week. I'm turning in.

Hal: Me too.

(Lance looks around confused)

Lance: So what am I supposed to use as a pillow?

Hal & Buck: The mess of your thoughts.

Lance: How 'bout a blanket?

Hal & Buck: The light of the moon.

Lance: (*sniff!*) I want my Mommy!

Hal: Cut it out and go to sleep…cowboy.

Scripture reference: Matthew 6: 5-6 "And when you pray, do not be like the hypocrites, for they love to pray standing in the synagogues and on the street corners to be seen by men. I tell you the truth, they have received their reward in full. But when you pray, go into your room, close the door and pray to your Father, who is unseen. Then your Father, who sees what is done in secret, will reward you."

25. BOB AND BOB'S HILLBILLY JUG BAND (a skit on making a joyful noise)

Players:	*Two*; Bob and his brother Bob
Props:	Bob and Bob's costumes (ragged overalls, fake ugly teeth, straw hats)
	A large apple juice jug with "XXX" written across the front
	A bucket, a broomstick and a piece of string stretching from the top of the broomstick to the bucket to make an upright bass.

Character analysis: Bob and Bob are hillbillies from somewhere in the back woods. They both have hearts of gold and are slow to anger. When it comes to being friendly Bob and Bob know how to treat a stranger. What they are lacking is a general education beyond the third grade and a grasp on the finer points regarding personal hygiene.

Opening scene: Bob and Bob enter and set up their instruments, addressing the crowd in a Sunday church service.

BOB AND BOBS HILLBILLY JUG BAND

Bob #1: Mornin' bretherin! I'm Bob and this is my brother Bob...

Bob #2: Greet'n y'all.

Bob #1: An' we's been asked by yer pastor to lead y'all in worship today and maybe some other jibber-jabber.

Bob#2: I don't reckon y'all praise n' worship like we do back home but we are happier'n a wood grub in a dead oak tree to broaden yer horizons a smidgen.

Bob #1: It's just like our momma and daddy, Bob and Bobbi Roberts always says, "the Lord don't care if yer one of those prissy opera singers or a cricket in a wood pile, all praise to God is beautiful music."

Bob#2: That's right, Bob, so let's get to pickin'. We'd better tune our instruments though.

(Bob #1 plucks the one string on his bucket/broom bass)

Bob #2: Mighty nice.

(Bob #2 blows into his jug)

Bob#1: Beau-ti-ful!

Bob#2: Let's give 'em all we got.

(The two hillbillies begin to play and sing the words "praise the Lord" over and over to the tune of "Oh Suzanna")

Bob and Bob: Praise the praise the praise the praise the praise the praise the praise the Lord! Praise the praise the praise the praise the praise the praise the praise the Lord! Praise the praise the, oh praise the praise the Lord.

Praise the praise the praise the praise the praise the praise the praise the Lord! Amen!

Bob #2: (responding to the applause) Thank y'all!

Bob#1: I'm feelin' good now Bob!

(The two Bob's break into song again using the same tune but these different words.)

Bob and Bob: I'm-a-feelin' feelin' feelin' feelin' feelin' feelin' good! I'm-a-feelin' feelin' feelin' cause I love Christ like I should. Praise the praise the praise the praise the praise the praise the lord! We love this tune, it's endin' soon we hope you ain't too bored!

Bob and Bob: (in response to the applause) Thank y'all. Bye now!

Scripture reference: Psalms 100: 2 "Worship the Lord with gladness; come before Him with joyful songs."

26. BOB AND BOB'S HILLBILLY JUG BAND ANSWERING SERVICE (a skit on always doing your best)

Players:	Three; Bob, his brother Bob, and someone off stage who will imitate the sound of a telephone ringing.
Props:	Bob and Bob's costumes (ragged overalls, fake ugly teeth, straw hats)
	A large apple juice jug with "XXX" written across the front
	A bucket, a broomstick and a piece of string stretching from the top of the broomstick to the bucket to make an upright bass
	A table and a telephone.

Character analysis: Bob and Bob are hillbillies from somewhere in the back woods. They both have hearts of gold and are slow to anger. When it comes to being friendly, Bob and Bob know how to treat a stranger. What they are lacking is a general education beyond the third grade and a grasp on the finer points regarding personal hygiene.

Opening scene: Bob and Bob appear with their instruments standing by a table with a telephone on it.

BOB AND BOB'S HILLBILLY JUG BAND ANSWERING SERVICE

Bob #1: For all's of you'n whose been missing us, we're here to tell you that Mamma grounded us from our instruments for a time but were back now and you'll be proud as a pigeon to know that we've secured ourselves a job.

Bob #2: We be telephone operators.

Bob#1: No we ain't Bob! We be telephone answerers, there's a big difference! One's more prestigious. An' who knows, maybe if we do a good job, we might even get paid.

Bob#2: Right, but we ain't doin' this job for the money.

Bob#1: Nope, we do our best in everything we do because that's what God says to do. Even if we were being paid as much as five cents an hour, we wouldn't walk around with our noses in the air.

Bob #2: Like a she-swine at slop time.

Bob#1: No, we work for God.

(RING, RING beckons a phone)

Bob#1: Golly, Bob, It's our first customer!

(The two Bob's fumble around until Bob#2 answers the phone.)

Bob#2: Bob and Bob's hillbilly jug band answering service…(*then, while covering the mouthpiece of the phone with his hand he continues*) its Dr. Meredith Stein!

Bob #1: Put her on hold!

Bob #2: One moment please.

(Bob and Bob lay the phone down on the table, and then they gather their instruments and sing the following words to the tune of "Macho Man".)

Bob and Bob: Matzo matzo ball, I want to be, a matzo ball. Matzo matzo ball, I want to be a Matzo!

(Bob #2 then picks the phone back up.)

Bob #2: What's that Dr. Stein? (*He covers the mouth piece again and speaks to Bob#1*) She says that she's coming over here to give us a spankin'!

Bob #1: Hang up on her!

Bob #2: We ain't got any messages for you, bye now. (*Bob #2 then hangs up the phone*)

(RING, RING! Bob and Bob fumble over the phone again.)

Bob #1: Bob and Bob's hillbilly jug band answering service…(*Bob #1 covers the mouth piece and speaks to Bob#2*) It's Helga and Inga Weisberg!

Bob #2 Put them on hold!

Bob #1: But I don't know any German music!

Bob #2: It can't be too hard; all they ever say is "Ach!"

(Bob and Bob lift their instruments and sing the word "Ach!" repeatedly to the tune of "Twinkle, Twinkle Little Star".)

Bob and Bob: Ach ach, ach ach, ach ach ach, ach ach, ach ach, ach ach ach. Ach ach, ach ach, ach ach ach, ach ach, ach ach, ach ach ach. Ach ach, ach ach, ach ach ach, ach ach, ach ach, ach ach ach! (*Then both Bob and Bob spit.*)

Bob #1: What's that? They're clappin'! They liked it! No Ma'am, they ain't any messages for y'all. (*Bob #1 then hangs up the phone.*)

(RING, RING! Both Bob's clamber over the phone once again Bob #2 answers.)

Bob#1: This is a great job!

Bob #2: (*answering confidently*) Bob and Bob's hillbilly jug…(*Bob gasps and covers the mouthpiece of the phone while speaking to Bob #1.*) It's MAMA!

(Bob #1 screams and bites his fingers.)

Bob #2: She's calling from the kitchen an' she says to quit playn' or she's going to go BOVINE on us!

Bob #1: Quick, hang up! She already sounds madder'n a mule!

(Bob #2 hangs up the phone.)

Bob #1: Well, I'm-a-guessin' were gonna be grounded from our instruments again…

Bob #2: Right, but soon as Mama lets us, we'll be back. Take care y'all!

Scripture reference: Col. 3: 23 "Whatever you do, work at it with all your heart, as working for the Lord, not for men, since you know that you will receive an inheritance from the Lord as a reward. It is the Lord Christ that you are serving."

27. MASTERCARD THEATER (a skit on the danger of debt)

Players:	Three; Gary, Brenda, and Reginald Swimminindebt III.
Props:	Large comfortable chair for Reginald
	Reginald's costume (pipe, dinner jacket)
	Small table and two chairs
	Papers and a calculator on top of the table
	A long accordion of credit cards all connected together in a folding strip.

Character analysis: Reginald Swimminindebt III is an upper crusty man raised amid great privilege. He has never had to wear the same dinner jacket twice nor has he ever had to work. He speaks with a British accent.

Gary and Brenda are a newly married couple with college degrees and hefty college loans to pay. They are seduced by the instant gratification that credit cards can bring.

Opening scene: the spotlight is on Reginald, who is sitting in his chair, smoking a pipe and looking pompous. To the side of him, Gary and Brenda are busy paying their bills at the kitchen table.

MASTERCARD THEATER

Reginald: Greetings, and welcome to MasterCard Theater. I am your host, Reginald Swimminindebt the Third. Tonight, an American classic that you will all recognize entitled "Where Did All Our Money Go?" will captivate and enthrall you as our newlyweds Gary and Brenda Jones, portray the epic struggle between young love and needful things. So, sit back and prepare to enjoy "Where Did All Our Money Go?"

(Spotlight changes to couple at table)

Brenda: Gary, I just realized that there are four bills here that were due a month ago, that we never sent.

Gary: Oh boy, let's see. *(Gary reaches for the bills in Brenda's hand)* Electricity, water, garbage and cable TV. Those are pretty important, but we've got to pay our credit card premiums first before we pay anything else or all of our stuff will be repossessed.

Brenda: It's going to be a tough month without water or electricity. But we'll survive. I love you honey!

Gary: I love you too dumpling, hey look, another pre-approved credit card from Sell-Your-Soul credit lines.

Brenda: Ooh, let me see. *(She takes the brochure)*

Gary: It says effective immediately, twenty-five thousand dollars credit!

Brenda: Great! Now I can get that new do-it-yourself deck that I just loved down at the lumber store.

Gary: Heck, with that kind of money, we could add on too. I'll just be slipping this into my credit card directory, *(Gary unfolds a long accordion of fifty or so credit cards.)* Let's see, right here under "S" for "Sell-Your-Soul".

Brenda: Oh Gary, you're such a good provider!

(DING, DONG beckons the doorbell)

Brenda: That must be our new hot tub, dish washer and washer and dryer that I ordered from Sears. (*Brenda hops up from the table and leaves momentarily to answer the door.*)

Gary: Ahhh, I can't wait to settle into those warm bubbles under the moon-light.

Brenda: (*speaking from off stage*) Just leave everything here in the garage guys. Thanks! (*Brenda re-enters and catches Gary daydreaming.*) What's on your mind Gary?

Gary: Oh I'm just thinking about how nice it's going to be to sit in our hot tub tonight.

Brenda: Not only that! Goodbye dishpan hands! Hello deluxe dishwasher! No more trips to the laundromat for me, we've got a washer and dryer now.

Gary: Which card did you use for those, by the way?

Brenda: The blue one, or maybe it was the white. I don't remember exactly.

Gary: That's okay.

Brenda: Well should we get started? I've got dishes to clean!

Gary: And I've got some soaking to do!

(*The two excitedly turn to go but stop and face each other*)

Gary and Brenda: Oh…wait.

Brenda: Yes…the overdue water and electricity bills, if we don't pay those, we have no water and even if we did, we'd have no electricity to heat it with.

Gary: Right, but we can't pay them because we have to pay the credit card that bought us all this stuff.

(*Gary and Brenda return to the table and sit*)

Brenda: I think we're in trouble.

Gary: Yes, I think you're right about that.

(Spotlight returns to Reginald)

Reginald: Wasn't that moving? The poor young naves had all the gadgets they ever wanted but no way to make them work. Hee hee. Life can be so cruel to the under-privileged.

(Two guys—who resemble Bob and Bob—come in, pick up the chair that Reginald is in and begin to carry him off)

Reginald: What's this? I do say, what is the meaning of this? Put me down this minute!

Bob: Sorry Mr. Swimminindebt Sir, but you haven't paid yer bills in three months and me n' Bob here have come to repossess yer chair.

Reginald: (as he is being carried away) Wait! There must be some mistake.

Bob: Ya' know Bob, this job ain't as easy as playin' in the jug band.

Scripture reference: Romans 13: 8 "Let no debt remain outstanding, except the continuing debt to love one another, for he who loves his fellow man has fulfilled the law."

Matt. 6: 24 "No one can serve two masters. Either he will hate the one and love the other, or he will be devoted to one and despise the other. You cannot serve both God and money."

28. DON'T KNOW WHAT YOU GOT (a skit on taking God's grace for granted)

Players:	Six; Aaron, Sandy, angel, two demons and the announcer.
Props:	Aaron and Sandy—regular clothes
	Angel—angel costume and a book of life
	Special Music—"Don't Know What You Got, Till It's Gone" by Cinderella
	Haunting music of any kind
	Costume and face paint for two demon helpers

Flashlights and colored paper to create the look of "fire" on a nearby wall

Character analysis: Aaron is selfish, irresponsible and self-centered.

Opening scene: *Couple in a car—dating. As they drive, the guy (Aaron) isn't paying attention to the girl (Sandy) instead he's looking out the window at other girls and his friends—girl is getting annoyed—hip hop music playing.*

DON'T KNOW WHAT YOU GOT

Announcer: Have you ever taken anyone for granted?

Aaron: Yo babe—hey Jo Jo, wha'sup bro? All right, yeah, I got it going on. Yo, yo, yo Bradster—Ooh la la honey—hey how's it going?

Sandy: There's something I need to tell you, Aaron. I'm breaking up with you.

Aaron: (*doesn't listen keeps looking out window, checks his look in mirror*) Shake that bootie, Uh huh that's right—raise the roof, ha ha ha. (*Suddenly, he notices that Sandy has said something to him*) What was that Babe?

Sandy: I said, it's over! I'm tired of you taking me for granted. You don't even pay attention to me while we're together. I'm just an ornament on your arm. It's over! I'm tired of being used!

Aaron: Listen Sandy, I'm sorry, don't leave—you mean everything to me!

Sandy: Too little, too late, Aaron. I'm going to find someone who really cares.

(*Sandy jumps out of car*)

Aaron: No! Sandy, no! I can't go on without you! Don't make me an old lonely man!

(*"Don't Know What You Got Till its Gone" by Cinderella begins to play or any forlorn love song*)

Aaron: (*Sob! Sob!*) I didn't even see it coming…I've been so wrong! (*Sob! Sob!*) At least I'm still young! Oh hey, there's Kristy. Yeah Baby, let's get to know each other. I'm a single man now!

Announcer: We've all taken some things for granted whether it was our friends or our parents or our health. But, what about God? God forgives us time after time for taking Him for granted. He forgives us for all the evil and thoughtless things we've done to Him or to others when we ask with a contrite heart. But God's forgiveness isn't to be taken lightly. Knowing you can be forgiven eventually, sometime before you die isn't a good enough excuse to keep ignoring Him and His laws. What if your life ended unexpectedly before you had a chance to repent?

(Aaron leaves his car and approaches angel with book)

Aaron: Where am I?

Angel: Greetings. You are just outside the gates of heaven. Name please?

Aaron: All right! I always heard God was forgiving. Boy, He must be! I haven't thought about God or anyone but myself for years, ha ha! I still made it—cool! Oh, my name is Aaron Jones. I must have died, huh? What's that book anyway?

Angel: It's the Book of Life. All who have asked for forgiveness of their sins and given their lives to the Lord have their names written in it. They are allowed into heaven.

Aaron: That's funny. I never asked for forgiveness. I mean I knew I was supposed to and everything, I just figured I had lots of time. You know, I wanted to have fun while I was young and worry about the after life when I was old and sick.

Angel: I'm sorry to inform you that your name doesn't appear in the Book of Life. You are not allowed into heaven.

(Angel points to a sea of fire being reflected on the wall with flashlights while haunting music plays)

Aaron: No, you can't be serious? I was going to repent! I promise I was, how was I s'post to know that I was going to die at 16 years old—I wasn't given enough chances! I wasn't given time to choose!

Angel: Your choice came when you knowingly turned away from Jesus Christ, rejecting Him. You then lived to serve yourself…

Aaron: But I was just living like everyone else.

Angel: You've sealed your own fate.

(Two demons appear and carry Aaron away)

Aaron: No! No! I'm sorry I took God for granted. I'll change!

Announcer: You see how important it is to be right with God, no matter what your age? Only God himself knows the number of our days. Giving your life and heart to Him now, choosing Him, is the best thing anyone could do for themselves and you'll be surprised at how much happier you are. God knows all your sins anyway. It's not like you can hide them from Him. Confess your heart to him. Give him a chance to work miracles in your life. Don't wait another minute. Do it today!

Scripture reference: Romans 10: 9 "That if you confess with your mouth, 'Jesus is Lord,' and believe in your heart that God raised him from the dead, you will be saved."

BIBLIOGRAPHY

1. Edward W. Goodrich and John R. Kohlenberger III, Donald L. Potts and James A. Swanson Asso. Editors.

The NIV Exhaustive Concordance. Grand Rapids, Mi.: Zondervan Publishing House, 1990

2. Philip Yancy and Tim Stafford. The Student Bible. Grand Rapids, Mi.: Zondervan Bible Publishers, 1986

3. Dr. Herbert Lockyear R.S.L. All The Women of the Bible. Grand Rapids, Mi.: Zondervan Publishing House, 1963

4. Dr. Herbert Lockyear R.S.L., F.R.G.S. All the Parables of the Bible. Grand Rapids Mi.: Zondervan Publishing House, 1963

5. Bruce Wilkenson and Kenneth Boa. Talk through the Old Testament. Nashville, Tenn., 1983

6. Bruce Wilkenson and Kenneth Boa. Talk through Bible Personalities. Nashville Tenn., 1983

ABOUT THE AUTHOR

Amy Bond, who lives in Baker City, OR, is a Dental Hygienist by trade, mother and wife by heart. She enjoys playing guitar and singing in her church worship band, playing golf, and fishing with her husband and two sons. Since childhood, she had always felt an inclination to write but didn't take it seriously until after her own children were born. She is also the author of, "The Soul Seekers."

0-595-27857-4

Printed in the United States
85607LV00006B/270/A